THE
END
OF
BROOKLYN

Books *by* Robert J. Randisi

Nick Delvecchio Novels

The End of Brooklyn *
The Dead of Brooklyn
No Exit from Brooklyn

Other Novels

The Bottom of Every Bottle *
You're Nobody 'Til Somebody Kills You
Hey There (You with the Gun in Your Hand)
Luck Be a Lady, Don't Die
Everybody Kills Somebody Sometime
Alone With the Dead
Arch Angels
East of the Arch
Blood on the Arch
In the Shadow of the Arch

Short Stories

The Guilt Edge *

Anthologies (Editor)

The Shamus Winner Volume I (1982-1995) *
The Shamus Winners Volume II (1996-2009) *
Hollywood and Crime
The Eyes Have It

* Published by PERFECT CRIME BOOKS

THE END OF BROOKLYN

ROBERT J. RANDISI

PERFECT CRIME BOOKS

Printed in the United States of America.

Perfect Crime Books is a registered Trademark.

Cover Image Elements @ 2011 by BigStock and iStockphoto. All rights reserved. Used by permission.

This book is a work of fiction. The characters, entities and institutions are products of the Author's imagination and do not refer to actual persons, entities, or institutions.

Library of Congress Cataloging-in-Publication Data
Randisi, Robert J.
The End of Brooklyn / Robert J. Randisi
ISBN: 978-1-935797-12-8

First Edition: June 2011

THE
END
OF
BROOKLYN

Prologue

BROOKLYNITES HAVE NO IMAGINATION.

For the most part, it's Florida for vacation, and Florida for retirement.

I wasn't on vacation, or retired.

I was hiding out.

And not in Florida.

Actually, that part about no imagination goes for most New Yorkers.

I was a native of Brooklyn, and a lifelong resident, until about fifteen years ago. Since then I'd been moving around, living in different places, doing odd jobs that had some connection to what I did for a living for years—I was a private detective.

These days I did jobs for people that didn't involve paying me with a check, because I didn't have any bank accounts.

I was spending the morning sitting on my deck with a cup of coffee, a forty-five, and looking at the Mississippi, which spread out panoramically below me. At fifty years old, the past fifteen years had not gone the way I might have thought. In my early thirties if you had told me I would live anywhere but Brooklyn I would have told you that you were crazy.

I certainly never would have expected to be living in a house in the Midwest, on a bluff above the most famous river in the world. I liked the isolation. The long driveway that led to the house from the main road was all gravel, which meant vehicles driving on it made a lot of noise. And the only vehicle that drove on it was the mail truck.

The gravel also crunched underfoot—my own security system. So when I heard that crunching sound, being caused by more than one set of feet, I knew they'd found me, and I was in trouble.

I wasn't finished with my coffee.

I tucked the forty-five underneath my left butt cheek, and waited. Running at this point was not an option. Besides, I'd been running for fifteen years. I was getting a little too old for it.

"Nick Delvecchio?"

I turned in the direction of the voice. Three men had come up the steps and onto my deck, which spread the entire width of the house. So at that moment they were about twenty feet from where I sat. I'd once come out on the short end of a shootout at this range.

"Who's asking?"

"I think you know," the spokesman said.

"I like to deal in names."

"Names don't really matter," he said, "but let's go with . . . John."

"I detect a Brooklyn accent," I said, "so I'll bet as a kid it was Johnny."

He didn't respond. He was about my age, probably grew up in a neighborhood like I did. The other two were younger, maybe late thirties. They weren't talkers. They looked Italian, but the spokesman had a different look to him.

"Are you Delvecchio?" John asked.

"I think you know I am."

"I need confirmation."

I shrugged. "Then I am."

John looked around.

"I can still hear a little of it in your voice."

"Most people can't."

"This is a long way from Brooklyn."

"You said it."

"That coffee?"

I nodded.

"Any more?"

"Inside," I said. "The kitchen. Have one of your . . . friends go and get it."

"Thanks."

He looked at one of them. The man went inside for a few moments, came out with a mug of coffee. Just one. That established the pecking order for me. I would only be talking to John.

I was sitting in a wrought iron chair, one of a set of four, at a matching table.

"You mind?" he asked, gesturing with the mug.

"Not at all."

He sat to my right, which meant he couldn't see the gun butt sticking out from beneath my ass.

"Nice out here in the fall," he said.

"Lots of bugs in the summer."

"Been here long?"

"Not that long."

"You've led us on a pretty good chase."

"You, personally?" I asked.

"Well, no," he said, "I meant . . ."

"I know what you meant."

He sipped his coffee, looked down at the river. The other two leaned against the railing. One watched me, one watched John.

"Parked down at the entrance to your road," John said. "Didn't want you to hear us drive up."

"I probably would've thought it was the mail man."

"Still . . ." he said, with a shrug.

"So what do we do now?" I asked.

"Well," he said, "there's what we're supposed to do, and then there's what I'd like to do."

"Are they very different?"

"Yeah, they are."

"What would you like to do?"

"Talk."

"And what're you supposed to do?"

"I think you know that, too."

"So," said, "let's talk."

"I'm curious," he said.

"About what?"

"About what happened fifteen years ago."

"Why?"

"Because I was around then," he said. "You wouldn't remember. I wasn't anybody at the time, but I was around. I know a little about what happened, but only the obvious stuff."

"So what do you wanna know?" I asked.

"Nick, I wanna know what happened," he said. "I wanna know what made you do what you did, and then bolt. Leave Brooklyn. Because I can't imagine leavin' Brooklyn. Just bein' out here among all the trees . . . I mean, it's nice and all . . . but I'd get the heebie jeebies after a while."

"Takes some gettin' used to," I said.

"So . . . you mind talkin' for a while?"

"Considerin' the alternative . . . not at all. Where would you like me to start?"

"Anyplace you feel comfortable startin'."

I looked at him for a minute, then asked, "You ever go to any of your high school reunions?"

One

Brooklyn, 1995

"I'M NOT GOING."

"Why not?" my neighbor, Samantha Karson, asked.

"Because it's stupid," I said. "I mean, come on. Eighteen years? Don't they usually have reunions at fifteen, and twenty? But eighteen?"

"Did you go to your fifteenth?" she asked.

"I didn't go to the tenth or the fifteenth," I said. "And I'm not going to the eighteenth—or, for that matter, the twentieth."

"Oh, come on," she said. "Don't you think your high school buddies will find you being a private eye exciting? Or the girl? Didn't you have a girl in high school?"

"I had lots of girls in high school," I admitted. "What I didn't have was a girlfriend."

"Braggart," she said.

She put the invitation down and picked up her turkey club. She was on another diet, which was why we had lunch together a few times a week. She said it helped her. She came across the hall and made us lunch. Today she had a turkey club while I just had a good old turkey sandwich—piled high!

She was a lovely, full-bodied blonde who, as far as I ever knew, was proud of that fact. Why then was she always trying to lose five pounds?

She took a bite of her sandwich and said, "I think you should go."

"Why?"

"Why shouldn't you go? Didn't you have some friends in high school?"

"Sure, I had *some* . . ."

"But not a lot?"

"A few."

"And no girlfriends?"

"Maybe one or two . . ."

"And aren't you curious about what's happened to them? What kind of adults they've become?"

"No."

"Why not?"

"I might be disappointed."

She stared at me, then asked, "Or maybe you think they'll be disappointed in you?"

Okay, so I decided to go to the damned thing.

The reunion was held in Marine Park, at a hall on Avenue N called the Something-or-other Chateau. A chateau in Brooklyn . . .

I admit to some nervousness as I walked through the front door. Brooklyn was a big place and although not many of us had left, we had spread out across the borough and hardly saw each other over the years. That suited me. High school was not something I thought back on fondly.

But as a huge apparition appeared in front of me, arms spread wide, I also admit to being glad to see him.

"Nicky-D!" he shouted, grabbing me in a bear hug and just about squeezing the life out of me.

"Tony Mitts!" I surprised myself by shouting back at him with almost as much enthusiasm.

It was then I silently thanked Sam for talking me into attending.

It was later that I cursed her for it . . .

Tony Mitts was just the start of the reunion. In rapid order I met up with Sammy Carter, Joey "the Nose" Bagaletti and Sal "the Ace" Pricci. The five of us used to hang out together in high school, which a lot of people found odd because while the rest of us were Italian, Sammy was black. We used to tell people he was "black" Italian. Among ourselves we also said that if anyone had a problem with him hanging out with us, "Fuck 'em!"

We staked out a place at the bar, watched the girls go by and talked about Gina Gershon making out with Elizabeth Berkley in *Showgirls* and the fact that the Yankees were going to finish second to Boston this year.

"But they're gonna get the wild card spot," Sal said. "Still gonna make the playoffs."

"Boy," Sammy said, "most of these girls have really porked up, huh?"

Showed you the difference between Sammy and Sal, one talking girls, the other baseball.

"What are you bitchin' about?" Tony said. "I thought skinny black guys like you liked your women with big asses."

Sammy fixed Tony with a hard stare. "You gonna start that 'fat-assed black girl' stuff again, Mitts? You were always doin' that in high school and I didn't like it then."

"Yeah, yeah . . ." Tony said.

It was true. This was an old argument from high school, but the rest of us knew that the two of them always secretly enjoyed the argument.

I examined my four high school friends. What I had told Samantha was close to the truth. In four years of high school I had made four friends. That counted as a few.

Tony had always been big, well over six feet, but he'd never been fat, and he still wasn't. He'd kept himself in remarkable shape, but then as an athlete he would. We called him "Tony Mitts" because he had hands the size of catcher's mitts. His real last name was Bologna, but our nickname was better than what they used to call him in junior high—"Tony Baloney." Ah, junior high kids had no imagination.

Sammy Johnson was as skinny as ever, but his hair had receded to the halfway point of his head. The bald part gleamed the way Lou Gossett's or George Foreman's did. I wondered why he didn't just shave it all off?

Sal had gone to fat, which he had always been leaning to in high school. His arms and shoulders still threatened to burst the seams of his clothes. We would have called him "the Arm" but Tony was "Mitts" and we didn't want another body part in the group. So, because of his affinity for cards—poker, mostly—we called him "the Ace."

Joey's nose was as big as ever, which had made his nickname very easy in high school. It was a family trait, he was always pointing out to us, and all the men in his family were proud of it.

"Anybody seen Mary Ann?" I asked.

Suddenly, Tony smiled.

"She's here," he said.

"Yeah," Sal said, slapping Tony on his broad back. "She came with Tony, the lucky dog."

"Man," Sammy said, "she looks good, even if she don't have an ass on her."

"You wanna see her?" Tony asked me. He was anxious.

"Sure."

I agreed not only because he was apparently so eager to show her off, but because I was curious. Mary Ann had been the best looking girl in our class—maybe in the whole school. I wondered what she looked like eighteen years later.

A couple of girls went by. I didn't recognize them, but they had adopted the new looks of bare, pierced belly buttons, and they shouldn't have.

"Come on." Tony grabbed my arm in an iron grip and dragged me across the floor.

I had never gotten to know Mary Ann Grosso well in high school, although I knew a lot of guys who bragged they had. They all claimed to have scored, too, except for Tony. He not only said he hadn't, but that nobody else had, either.

He pulled me over to a table where a bunch of people were sitting. I was able to pick Mary Ann out with no trouble. She was even more beautiful at thirty-six than she had been at eighteen. She'd grown into her beauty. She had dark hair that hung down to her shoulders. I recalled that she had always had beautiful skin—smooth and creamy and free of acne. She still did.

"Mary Ann, here's Nicky!" Tony said. When she frowned he said, "Come on, you remember, Nicky-D!"

"Of course," she said. "Nicky." I knew she wasn't lying. She remembered me, if not right away. She held out both hands warmly, and I took them. "It's good to see you."

"And you, Mary Ann. You look . . . great."

"Don't she though?" Tony blustered right over her soft, "Thank you." He was obviously very proud of her, and when he told me that they were to be married, I realized why.

By the following week, Mary Ann was dead.

Two

ALL DEATH IS TRAGIC.

Particularly when it's accidental. After all, someone dying as result of a fluke? An accident? Or an act of carelessness? Tragic, to say the least. Now natural causes, that's probably the least tragic of all—if you can use the words "least" and "tragic" in the same sentence. I mean, what can you do about that? A man goes to the doctor one week, is given a clean bill of health, and then drops dead the next week. Happens all the time, right?

So where does murder fit into the equation? Well, in my opinion, murder is just a step below accident. After all, what's tragic about one person taking the life of another? That's not tragic—it's just a damn shame!

And where does suicide fit in?

Who the hell knows.

I stared at the casket from my seat in the back of the chapel. I chose to sit there alone because I was not family. As a matter of fact, I was not even a close friend. I was someone who had known the deceased in high school, and then met her again one evening eighteen years later. And a week later, she's dead.

High school was not a favorite time of my life. I know people of varying ages who claim that, given the opportunity to go back in time, they'd go back to high school and do it all again. Best time of their lives. My opinion of people like that is they can't deal with having grown up.

Given the opportunity to go back to any time of my life, I'd choose to stay right where I am. That either means that this is the happiest time of my life, or I haven't had it, yet. I choose the latter. Why? It means I still have something to look forward to.

To me, looking forward is much better than looking back.

From my vantage point in the chapel I could see Tony Bologna's broad back. His shoulders were shaking. Sitting to his right was his mother. Her shoulders were ramrod straight. On his left was Mary Ann's mother. She was alternately patting and rubbing his back, the way I thought his own mother should have been doing.

I looked up toward the casket again, where Mary Ann Grosso was lying, all dressed up and made to look "good" in death. At my mother's funeral I would have throttled anyone who said aloud, "She looks *good*."

Mary Ann Grosso just looked dead.

After the service I decided not to accompany the family and friends to the cemetery. I stopped to tell Tony that and he grabbed my arm tightly.

"Come to Mary Ann's mother's house, Nicky."

"Tony," I said, "I don't want to intrude . . ."

"Her mother wants you there, Nick. She wants to talk to you."

"I didn't even think she remembered me."

"She doesn't; I told her you're a detective."

"Tony—"

"Please, Nick!" His eyes were as pleading as his tone.

"All right, Tony."

"Thanks, buddy." His relief was palpable. "We should get back to the house by two. Be there, okay? There'll be lots of food."

Of course there would. It was an Italian wake, after all.

"I'll be there."

I stood out in front of the funeral home and watched the procession leave. I became aware that someone was standing next to me.

"It's a damn shame, ain't it?" Sal asked. I hadn't seen him since the reunion, and hadn't noticed him inside.

"Yeah, it is." I looked at him. "I didn't see you inside."

"I didn't go in." He shook his head. "I couldn't. I didn't wanna see her like that."

"Are you going to the house?"

"Nah. You?"

I nodded. "Tony asked me to. Says her mother wants to talk to me."

"They gonna hire you, Nicky?"

"I'm afraid they're gonna try."

"Why afraid? Ain't that what you do? The private eye thing?"

"It's gonna be hard turning them down."

"Why turn them down?"

"I don't investigate suicides, Sal."

"Then there's no problem, Nicky." He slapped me on the back. "She didn't kill herself."

"How do you know that?"

"I knew her—I knew her as long and as well as Tony did. She'd never kill herself."

"Are you sayin' she was murdered?"

"I'm sayin' she wouldn't have killed herself, Nick. And that's *all* I'm sayin'."

"Sal—"

"Gotta go."

He moved away from me abruptly. I watched him walk to the parking lot and get into a new Chevy. I realized I didn't know what he did for a living. I'd pretty much talked to everyone else at the reunion about their jobs, but Sal had always seemed to avoid the subject.

I wondered if he'd meant to imply what I thought he'd been saying when he mentioned knowing Mary Ann as well as Tony did.

Three

I GOT TO THE HOUSE ABOUT TWO-THIRTY. IT WAS IN BENSONHURST, ON Sixty-Third Street. Actually, it was walking distance from my father's house, where I grew up. There was a new red '95 Pontiac Firebird in the driveway among some other, older cars.

"Nicky," Tony Mitts said, as I entered. "God." He came to me in the hall and clamped down on my arm again. "I thought maybe you weren't comin'."

"I said I would. Take it easy, Tony."

"I been tryin' to take it easy, Nick, but it ain't that easy. You don't *know . . .*"

"Don't know what?"

"Look, lemme tell Mary Ann's mother you're here. Get somethin' to eat and I'll find you. Get a beer. Okay?"

He was talking a mile a minute and was gone before I could reply. I went looking for a beer and found one in the kitchen. I also found a girl crying. It took me a minute, but I recognized her as Catherine, Mary Ann's little sister. Well, maybe not so little, but younger. If I remembered correctly Catherine was about two or three years behind us in high school. She was never as pretty as her sister, but she seemed to have grown into it. She had the same smooth, pale skin.

She was sitting at the kitchen table, clutching a handkerchief and crying softly. I had taken a St. Paulie Girl from the refrigerator when I turned and noticed her.

"Hey, I'm sorry."

She looked up at me, hastily wiping the moisture away from her eyes. She frowned, trying to place me.

"Catherine, I'm Nick—"

"Delvecchio," she said. "I remember. I had a terrible crush on you in high school. But you were a senior and I was a freshman." She blurted it out, then slapped her hand over her mouth.

"Did you?" I said. "I never knew."

She took her hand away from her mouth and said, "Nobody did—except Mary Ann."

There was an awkward silence then, which she broke.

"It's nice of you to come, Nick," she said. "I didn't think you'd remember . . . us."

"Well," I said, "I was at the reunion . . . I saw Mary Ann . . . and the guys."

"Wasn't she beautiful?" she asked, her eyes shining from both tears and pride. "Even more than she was in high school."

"Well, yeah, she was," I said, not really knowing how to answer. What did she want me to say? She seemed sincere, but I had two older brothers, and I wasn't always thrilled about it. Were there times, I wondered, when she didn't idolize her older sister so much?

"I can't believe she's gone," she said, starting to sob into her hanky again. "Not . . . not like that."

It occurred to me then that I still didn't know exactly how Mary Ann had died.

"Nick, there you are," Tony said bursting into the room. He didn't even seem to notice Catherine. "Come on, Mrs. Grosso wants to talk to you."

"In a minute, Tony. Catherine, are you all right?"

"I'm fine, Nick." She waved her hand. "Go ahead, ma wants you."

"Why don't we talk some more later?" I asked.

"Sure, Nick," she said with a small smile. "Why not?"

"Come on, Nick!' Tony said, impatiently grabbing my arm.

Old friend or not I was tired of having my arm mangled.

"Tony, damn it, take it *easy*, okay? I'm coming."

I jerked my arm away and he released it like it was hot.

"Sorry."

"Lead the way."

I followed him down the hall.

Four

TONY TOOK ME PAST A COUPLE OF BEDROOMS TO A ROOM AT THE END OF the hall. Inside Mrs. Grosso was sitting on a bed, staring out the window. What she was seeing what anybody's guess.

From the looks of the room it was a girl's—probably Mary Ann's old room. Or did she still live here. I didn't know.

A photo on a nearby dresser, confirmed my suspicion that this had, at least once, been Mary Ann's room. It was her and Tony, arms around each other, laughing. From the looks of the scene behind them it was Coney Island—certainly happier times. It also looked to be an older picture, not one from high school, but certainly not much later.

"Mrs. Grosso?" Tony said.

For a moment she didn't seem to hear him, but then she turned her head and looked at us. I wondered how old she was. Sixty? Sixty-five? She was still an attractive woman, definitely Mary Ann and Catherine's mother. She had the same skin. I remembered Tony telling me she had lost her husband five years before. Now Mary Ann. All she had left was Catherine.

"Tony." Her voice was so hoarse we barely heard her.

"This is Nick Delvecchio, Mrs. Grosso," Tony said, awkwardly. Obviously, even though he was going to marry her daughter, he hadn't gotten around to calling her anything more personal. "He went to school with us."

"Yes," she said, "I know, Tony. I remember Nick. How's your father?"

"He's fine, Mrs. Grosso."

"I see him on the street sometimes," she said. "He's gone through a lot, with the death of your brother, and your sister being on that hijacked plane."

"He's come through it all with flying colors, Mrs. Grosso."

"Good, that's good," she said. "I came through my husband's death, but this . . . I don't know how I can come through this."

"You still have Catherine, Mrs. Grosso."

"Yes," she said, "I still have Catherine."

"Tell him about Mary Ann, Mrs. Grosso," Tony said, anxiously. "Tell him Mary Ann didn't—"

"Tony." She interrupted him. "Can I talk to Nick alone, please?"

He looked as if she had slapped him in the face.

"But—I thought—"

"Please, Tony?"

"Oh, well . . . sure, Mrs. Grosso, sure . . ."

Tony gave me a puzzled glance, then backed out of the room.

"He's a nice boy," she said.

"Yeah, he is."

"Would you close the door please, Nick?"

"Sure."

"And come sit here by me," she said, as I closed it. She patted a spot next to her and I noticed for the first time a folder there. When I sat the folder was between us.

"Mrs. Grosso—"

"Please," she said, "call me Angela. It's actually Angelina, but that's too long, don't you think? And too . . . old country?"

"It's a very pretty name."

"Yes, well . . . when I was in high school they called me 'Angel.' Isn't that silly?"

"Mrs.—uh, Angela, can we talk about Mary Ann?"

"Of course. My Mary Ann," she said. "They say she killed herself."

"Who says so, Angela?"

"The police."

"Can you tell me how she died?"

"She died right here," she said, touching the mattress, "on this bed."

"But *how* did she die?"

"Pills," she said. "She took pills . . . that's what they told me."

"Suicide."

Angela Grosso nodded.

"But Tony doesn't believe it," I said.

"Tony was very much in love with Mary Ann, Nick. He refuses to believe it."

"And you?"

"Mary Ann was . . . troubled."

"Angela—"

"Here." She picked up the folder and handed it to me.

"What's this?"

"Poems," she said. "My Mary Ann's poems."

"Poems?" I said.

"How well did you know my daughter, Nick?"

"Not well," I admitted. "We went to school together, but after we graduated I sort of lost touch . . . with everybody . . ."

"Mary Ann wrote these poems," she said, tapping the folder. "In all these years since high school, she's written these poems. She even had some published in magazines."

"That's, um, nice."

"You don't understand," she said. "You would have to read these poems to understand. The girl who wrote these poems . . . the *woman* . . . was troubled."

"Mrs. Grosso, Tony said you wanted to talk to me about—"

"I told him I didn't, Nick. He wants me to hire you to prove that Mary Ann did not commit suicide . . . but I believe she did. Read the poems, and you'll see."

"All right, Mrs. Grosso. I'll read them."

I left, taking the folder with me. Tony was waiting for me in the hall.

"Did she do it? Did she hire you?"

"No, Tony, she didn't."

He firmed his jaw and said, "Then I want to, Nick. I want you to prove Mary Ann didn't do it. She wouldn't commit suicide. Those are her poems. They're beautiful,. You read them and see."

"I'll read them Tony, and then I'll get back to you."

Angela Grosso thought the poems meant Mary Ann committed suicide. Tony thought they proved otherwise. Now I was curious about them.

Five

"SO WHAT DID YOU TELL HIM?" SAM ASKED.

We were in my apartment, sharing a pizza she had shown up at my door with only moments after I had returned from the Grosso funeral. Far be it for me to turn away a beautiful woman *with food*.

"What could I tell him?" I asked. "I took the poems and told him I'd read them."

She looked at the folder on the table, and then looked at me. She had her hair pulled back and secured with a "scrunchie." Scrunchies were all the rage, and I hated them.

"Can I read them, too?"

"Well, duh," I said. "You're the writer. I was hoping you'd read them and tell me what you think."

Samantha "Kit" Karson had been writing Romance novels for a few years, and had only recently turned to writing mysteries. Actually, she says they're called "Romantic Suspense."

"What did they tell you about the poems?" she asked.

"The mother says once I read them I'll know she killed herself. Tony says once I read them I'll know she didn't."

"Well, they're either very depressing," Sam said, "or very uplifting."

"Can they be both?" I asked.

She shrugged and said, "I guess that's what we're going to find out."

THERE WERE hundreds of poems—eighteen years' worth, and after reading half a dozen each Sam and I exchanged a look, and then traded.

"Well?" I asked after we'd read those.

"God," she said, "these *are* depressing. The girl who wrote these was so . . . sad!"

I hated to admit it, but I agreed. Anyone who could write "Angel of Death," "Last Request," and "Midnight Crisis," not to mention something called "Laying Down To Die," *was* more than just sad.

"Listen to this line from 'Midnight Crisis,'" Sam said. "'Raindrops kiss my black lapels, then weep into my chest.'" She looked at me and said, "It's so beautiful . . . yet sad."

"You're the writer," I said, again. "Are these good?"

We were seated across from each other on the floor with the poems strewn out between us.

"These are . . . wonderful! I'm no poet, but . . . I wish I could write with this much beauty and passion."

"But they're sad."

"Well, maybe not all sad. Listen to this. It's from 'Laying Down To Die.' 'She's blind to the jelly bean colors, of balloons on a turquoise sky.'"

"That's great," I said, "but does it all mean she killed herself or not?"

"What if writing it down, writing down all the sadness she felt, was her way of dealing with it, of getting it out. What if she wrote it to keep from committing suicide? It could have been some sort of rite of expiation on her part."

"If you're gonna flaunt something could you make it something other than your writer's vocabulary? Like your body?"

She made a face.

"So, in her own mind, writing this all down would prevent her from having to commit suicide?" I asked.

"Maybe."

"So Tony's not just seeing something he wants to see," I said. "You think that two different people reading these poems could interpret them differently?"

"Well, I think you can always get differing opinions, don't you?"

I looked down at the poems on the floor, shifted them around, then heaved a big sigh.

"What?" she asked.

"I think she took her own life."

"So what are you gonna do?"

"Ask some questions," I said. "Maybe, if I can find out why, I can put her mother's mind at peace."

"I don't know how a woman who has lost a child can be at peace."

"You're probably right."

"So you're not going to treat this like it's a murder?" she asked.

"I can't," I said. "I don't see it that way."

She shrugged. "Maybe somebody poisoned her."

I shook my head. "I think that's your writer's imagination at work."

"All right," she said, getting to her feet. She was wearing a big floppy sweatshirt and a pair of jeans. Her feet were bare, since she'd only had to walk from across the hall. I noticed—not for the first time—that she had pretty feet.

"All right what?"

"Look into it any way you want," she said, "as long as you look into it."

I stood up, too.

"I have to go," she said. "I have twenty pages to do tonight and I've still got to watch Murphy Brown."

"Has all this talk about murder and suicide inspired you?"

"As a matter of fact," she said, as I walked with her to the door, "it has. I'll be up well past midnight if you want to talk more, or get a snack."

"I'll let you know." I looked back at the poems on the floor. "You want to take some of these with you?"

"No," she said, "you better finish reading them. Read as many as you can, Nicky. Maybe it'll help you see something definite."

As she went out the door I thought I already knew something definite. Mary Ann Grosso had been one very depressed girl.

I guess what I needed to find out was why.

I read some more, but at one point I just had to stop. Jesus, I was getting depressed and I'm normally a happy fella. Ask anybody.

I put the poems away in the folder and went to bed around midnight. Let Sam get her own snack.

Six

THE NEXT MORNING I GOT UP LATE AND LEAFED THROUGH THE POEMS again while I drank my coffee. I didn't have the heart to start reading again, though, because they would have taken the heart right out of me. I left the folder on my desk and decided to talk to people who knew Mary Ann Grosso a lot better than I did.

I started with Catherine. I called her at home and convinced her to have lunch with me. She agreed, but told me to come to the house at noon and she'd make something. That left me an hour to work with. I decided to talk to the police and see what they had on Mary Ann.

I made some calls, invoked the name of a friend and got the investigating detective to agree to talk to me.

His name was Detective Harry Nolan, and he worked out of the Sixty-Second Precinct.

"What have you got for me, Mr. Delvecchio?" he asked.

"Actually, I was hoping you'd have something for me, detective," I said. "I have two people trying to hire me. One thinks Mary Ann committed suicide, and one thinks she didn't."

"Well, all I've got for you is this: The M.E. says she died from a massive ingestion of sleeping pills. There were no signs of violence on the body, no signs that she'd been held down and fed the pills."

"What about the presence of other drugs?"

"Nada," he said, "not even aspirin, or birth control. She appeared to have simply taken all the pills, and then laid down to die."

The irony of that statement did not escape me.

"Did you find the pill container?"

"Yes. There was one in the upstairs master bathroom. They were the mother's pills. The daughter must have taken the pills, left the bottle in the sink, and then walked to bed. And then there was the note."

"What?" That was the first I'd heard of it. "What note?"

"The one they found clutched in her hand."

"What did it say?"

"I don't know," the detective admitted, "the title had something to do with suicide."

"Title?" I grabbed the folder, went through it.

There were several with suicide in the title. I read them off to him.

"That's the one. She had it in her hand."

"I'd like to see it."

"It's in evidence," he said.

"If I come in can you show it to me?"

"I suppose so."

"I'll call first," I said, "let you know I'm coming."

"Okay."

"I might not be in till later today."

"I'll be here."

"Is the case still open?" I asked.

He hesitated, then said, "Technically. We're just tying up loose ends, but . . ."

"You're buying suicide."

"Yes."

"Okay, Detective," I said. "Thanks."

Why hadn't Mary Ann's mom or Tony told me about the note?

I was reading the poem when there was a knock on the door. I opened it; Sam was standing there.

"What are you doing up?" I asked. "I thought you worked till late."

"I did, but I wanted to see if you read any more of the poems."

"I'm reading one now," I said, waving it. "Listen to this. 'Eyelids covering forever her pain, beating heart eternally resting.' She had this, or something like it, in her hand."

"Which one is it?"

"It's called 'Suicidal Daydream,'" I said. "What do you think about that?"

Seven

WHEN I GOT TO THE GROSSO HOUSE CATHERINE HAD MADE SOME SOUP and sandwiches. She also looked as if she had dressed for a date. She had her midriff showing, belly button pierced with a gold stud. I hoped I hadn't given her the wrong idea. Actually, she looked very pretty . . .

"Nick," she said, when we were seated at the table, "Tony told me he hired you."

"He thinks he hired me," I said. She looked puzzled. "I'm not going to bill him, Catherine."

"Well . . . that's very nice of you . . . but what can you do for him . . . us?"

"I don't know," I said, honestly. "Do you feel the way he does about Mary Ann's death, or do you agree with your mother?"

She opened her mouth to answer, but her voice seemed to fail her. There were two glasses of water on the table. She took a sip from one, either because her mouth was dry, or she was buying time to think.

"I don't know how I feel, Nick," she said, finally. "I mean, sometimes I'm absolutely numb."

"Do you think that someone might have killed your sister?"

"My God," she said, shaking her head. She held her hands up, as if she was going to cup her head between them, but instead she just held them there. "It sounds so ludicrous when you say it out loud like that. Who'd want to kill Mary Ann? And why?"

She reached out suddenly and grabbed my hand.

"Nick, do you actually think somebody killed my sister?"

"No, Catherine, I don't," I said. "I'm sorry, but I believe she committed suicide."

I took "Suicidal Daydreams" from my pocket and held it out to her.

"What's this?"

"This is the poem they found in her hand. The police consider it a suicide note."

She unfolded the page and read it, then let her hand drop to the table, holding the poem loosely.

"Do you know when she wrote that?" I asked.

Her face reddened.

"Catherine . . ."

"Yes."

"When?"

She touched her forehead with her left hand, as if she had a headache.

"Catherine?" I made my voice firmer.

"A couple of years ago," she said, finally.

"Did she talk about suicide then?"

She lifted her eyes to look at me. They were shiny with tears.

"It's not about suicide, Nick."

"Come on," I said, "look at the title. What else could it be about?"

"Look at the last line of the first stanza." She smoothed the page out on the table.

"'Damaged goods denied final blessing,'" I read.

"And the second stanza."

I looked at the last line of the second stanza and read, 'Remains of a deadly assault.'"

"Don't you see?" she asked. "'Damaged goods?' 'Deadly Assault?'"

"What are you trying to tell me, Catherine?"

"Nick . . ."

Suddenly it came to me.

"Catherine . . . are you telling me Mary Ann was raped?"

She nodded, tears streaming down her face.

"When? By who?"

"She never told anyone," she said. "Anyone but me."

"Why not?" I asked. "Why didn't she tell your mother?"

Her eyes widened. "Oh God, Nick, she would never have told Ma. She would have thought . . . Mary Ann was dirty."

"No," I said, "your mother would have helped her—"

"You don't know my mother, Nick," she said. "If she ever found out about this it would disgrace her. She would . . . would . . ."

She'd what, I wondered. Whatever she was thinking she couldn't say it out loud.

"Nick, haven't you wondered why Tony and Mary Ann are getting married—*were* just getting married now, after all these years?"

"Well . . . yeah, I wondered . . . a little."

"Mary Ann's led kind of a wild life, Nick," Catherine said. "She's not—wasn't—the nice little Catholic girl that . . . well, she's not . . ."

Was she going to say, " . . . the nice little Catholic girl that I am?"

"She's been . . . promiscuous in the past, but now she was ready to settle down, and Tony—he's loved her all these years, and he was ready to marry her."

"Who was it, Catherine?" I asked. "Who raped her?"

"She told me," Catherine said, "but . . . do you think he killed her? I mean, it was two years ago and she . . . she forgave him, Nick. Can you imagine? So why would he kill her now?"

"I don't know, Catherine," I said. "Why don't you let me go and ask him?"

Eight

SAL PRICCI LIVED IN THE OLD NEIGHBORHOOD, NOT FAR FROM WHERE
Mary Ann grew up and died, and where my father now lived. I walked
a block of identical two-family, brick, semi-attached homes, and then a
block filled with a couple of pizzerias, a donut shop, travel agent's
office, Chinese takeout, deli/grocery store, and newsstand. A couple of
kids with dirty knees, elbows and faces almost ran into me, then
ducked between parked and double-parked cars, chasing each other.
Two teenagers shouted remarks at a pretty, big-boobed blonde who
came out of one of the pizza places and got into her double-parked car
while ignoring them. A couple of old pensioners ran into each other
and stopped to shoot the shit. These were normal Brooklyn blocks, but
I bet none of these normal neighborhood people knew what had been
going on in Mary Ann Grosso's life.

Sal actually lived in his father's house, since both parents had
passed away. He had no brothers or sisters, which was unusual for
someone of our generation. When I was a kid I didn't have many
friends who were only children. That's what happens when you grow
up Catholic and Italian.

I didn't know if Sal was home or not, but I hoped he was. I wanted
to be able to wrap this case up quickly. I just found the whole thing too
depressing.

So I was hopeful when I rang the doorbell.

Sal came to the door.

"Nick," he said, surprised. He stared at me through the storm door, didn't unlock it. "What are you—it's good to see you."

"Can I talk to you, Sal?"

"Well . . . well, sure, come on in." He unlocked the door, backed away to allow me to enter.

He closed the door behind us and led me into the living room. The house was very much like Mary Ann's, very much like my father's. It's funny, I grew up in my father's house. It was my home for almost twenty years, but I always thought of it as my father's house.

"Can I get you a beer?" he asked. "Or . . . somethin'? I was watchin' ESPN. Fuckin' Mets are twenty games out."

"Braves are hard to beat," I said.

"Damn near impossible."

"No, drink, Sal. I just wanna talk."

"Sure. About what?"

"Mary Ann."

He frowned. "What about her? Did you find out anything about her suicide?"

"No," I said, "but I found out some other things."

He shuffled his feet uncomfortable and said, "Uh, what other things?"

"Come on, Sal," I said. "I think you know."

He shook his head slightly and said, "Uh, Nick, sorry, but I don't know—"

"I know about the rape, Sal."

"What?" he asked, his eyes widening. "No, whoa, wait a minute, there wasn't no rape, Nick. I don't know who you been talkin' to but—"

"I've been talking to someone Mary Ann confided in, Sal," I said, cutting him off.

"Jesus," he said, touching his face, "she didn't tell Tony that, did she?"

"I think if she had told Tony you'd know about it, Sal—you would have known two years ago, when it happened. He would've killed you."

"Nick," he said, "wait, let me show you something. All right? Before you say anything else."

Sal went into the dining room without waiting for an answer. He went to a hutch and opened a drawer. Just for a moment I wondered if he was going to come out of there with a gun, but instead he took a folded-up piece of paper and carried it back to me, leaving the drawer open.

"Here."

"What is it?"

"A poem," he said. "Mary Ann wrote it . . . for me. Read it."

I unfolded the paper and read the title: "You." I read the first stanza And saw that it was Mary Ann's voice, all right. I was starting to recognize her style.

"'Disappointments in life are many,'" it started. It was three stanzas, and the third finished with the line, "'Now I will be forever changed, refreshed, from loving you.'"

I looked at him. "Did she write this before the rape, or after, Sal?"

Sal stared at me for a few moments, and his eyes widened again. He said, horrified—and if he was acting he was damned good—"Jesus, you think I killed her!"

"Tell me what happened, Sal."

"Nick . . . look . . . I've been in love with Mary Ann for years, man. You know those stories we useta hear, about guys who scored with her?"

"Tony said they weren't true."

"Well, they were. I mean, I loved her, too, but I wasn't as blind as Tony was. He refused to believe those stories, but I knew they were true."

I didn't know what to say. If what Catherine said about her sister's promiscuity was true, it must have started in high school.

"So what does that mean, Sal, that she deserved—"

"No, you don't understand," he said. "Just listen." There was a look of desperation on his face, and in his eyes. "Tony wanted to marry her right out of high school, but she wasn't ready for that. She wanted to live her life, ya know? She traveled, she had affairs, one-night stands, but she always came back home. Tony and her mother, they kept treating her like she was a saint, but I knew different.

"I was always here, too, Nick, and always in love with her. Then, about three years ago, she came home and she was different. It was like she found God, or something. After all these years? It was like suddenly she *was* the saint Tony and her mother thought she was—but not quite. Even though she started to see Tony regularly, and they talked about marriage, all of a sudden she noticed me ya know? It was like a high school dream come true for me. We talked, we went places together, we did things . . . but we never had sex. She just wouldn't have sex with me. I couldn't understand that. She always told me I was the one keeping her sane, who knew her for what she was and still loved her. Tony, she said, loved who he thought she was. And her mother—well, Angela would never believe anything bad about her precious Mary Ann."

"So she wouldn't come across, huh?"

"It wasn't like that." He wiped away the sweat on his forehead with his palm. "I didn't want a quick fuck, Nick. I wanted to marry her, take care of her. I couldn't understand why she wouldn't make love with me."

"So you got tired of waiting?"

"Damn it, why won't you understand?" he shouted. "She came over here one day and gave me that poem, said she'd written it for me. I was blown away. Nobody'd ever done anything like that for me before. She . . . she let me kiss her, and then . . . then when things really started to heat up, she pushed me away . . . but she didn't push very hard ya know? I felt if I pressed her, if I insisted . . . and before you knew it we were on the floor . . . okay, so I tore her clothes a little . . . but I wouldn't call it rape, Nick. I'd never call it rape!"

"But she did, right?"

"Yeah," he said. Suddenly, it was as if all the strength had gone out of him. He sank into a chair and said, "Yeah, she did . . . but you know what? She said she forgave me. She understood."

"And?"

"And she said she never wanted to see me again . . . not like that. She said we were finished, even as friends."

"And you took that?"

"Sure, I took it," he said. "I loved her. I'd never hurt her."

I stared at him. I didn't know exactly what had happened between them that day. She called it rape. He didn't. Who knew? She told her sister it was rape, but was too ashamed to tell her mother.

He looked at me with anguished eyes. He wouldn't wait two years and then become angry enough to kill her, would he?

He hung his head and said, "I didn't kill her, Nick. I swear, I didn't . . . I didn't . . ."

I believed him.

By the time I left Sal's all I had was another reason Mary Ann might have committed suicide. Maybe the "rape" was weighing heavily on her mind, even after two years.

I went home, entered my place by the office door, rather than my living quarters. I had the biggest unit on the floor, so it had two entrances.

From the door I could see the message machine on my desk flashing. Odd, but when I think back to that moment later on it would seem to me that the light was flashing more urgently than usual. The red readout said there were six messages.

I pressed play, and my life changed.

Nine

WHEN I WENT THROUGH THE EMERGENCY ROOM DOORS BENNY WAS RIGHT there waiting for me. His face was covered with tears. I had never seen Big Benvenuto Carbone—Benny "the Card"—cry.

"They was havin' lunch, Nicky," he said, "at an outside table, ya know? And then it just happened. I was inside. When I come runnin' out they was just . . . lying there."

I put my hand on his big shoulder and said, "How are they, Benny?"

"They're workin' on them," he said. "Jeez, Nick, there was so much blood. I'm so sorry . . ."

"You've got nothing to be sorry about, bro," I said. I patted his shoulder and dropped my hand. "I'm gonna talk to somebody."

"Yeah, okay," he said, "they won't tell me nothin' 'cause I ain't related."

"Well, I am," I said, "so let's see what I can find out."

I left him there looking lost and went to the desk. The nurse was fifty-something, plain, and harried looking. There are two places in New York you never want to end up—Motor Vehicle, and any hospital emergency room. Both places are usually crowded, and that night was no exception.

I had to wait while a couple of people in front of me finished their business before I could step up to the counter.

"Yes?"

"My name is Delvecchio," I said. "My father and, uh, uncle were brought in, victims of gunshot wounds."

"Oh, yeah," she said. "They're being attended to right now."

"I'd like to talk to the doctor."

"The doctor will be with you as soon as he can."

"Well, at least you can tell me how they are?" I asked. "I really don't know anything."

"Actually, sir," she said, "there's nothing I can tell you. The doctor will be out—"

"Yes, I know," I said, "as soon as he can."

She gave me an exasperated look.

"Wouldn't you rather he do what he can for your father instead of coming out here and talk to you?"

"Okay, fine," I said, "you succeeded in making me feel this big." I held my forefinger and thumb an inch apart.

Her face softened.

"That wasn't my intention, sir. I'm sure the doctor will be out soon."

"Can you at least tell me . . . if they're alive?" I asked.

She looked around, then said, "They're alive, sir."

"Thanks."

I walked back to where Benny was still standing.

"Let's sit down, Benny."

We went over to a couple of orange plastic chairs and sat down. Benny's bulk threatened to flatten his chair, but it held. Because of how big he was I had to leave an empty chair between our two. There were a few other chairs empty, but those were the only ones where we could sit together.

"Benny?"

"I'm sorry, Nick," he said. "I just . . . can't get it together."

He was right. I'd never seen the big man so out of it. I was wondering why I was so calm, but I had a feeling it was because Benny was falling apart. I probably had him to thank for the fact that I wasn't a basket case. Especially since I didn't know how close or far from death my old man was.

"Benny," I said, "come on, man. Just tell me what happened."

"I tol' you," Benny said, shaking his head, "They were having lunch at Rizzo'd in the Bay, sittin' outside, when I heard the shots."

"Where were you?"

"Inside," Benny said, "I was sittin' inside. I shoulda been outside, but the Don said they wanted to talk."

"You gotta do what the Don says, Benny," I reminded him. "Then what?"

"I ran outside and there was a car speedin' away. It was a drive-by, Nick. A goddamned drive-by."

"How bad were they hit, Benny?"

"They was each hit a few times," he said. "I tried to put pressure on the wounds with napkins." He looked straight at me then, his eyes shining with tears. "I'm sorry, Nick. I—I went to the Don first."

I patted him on the shoulder and said, "It's okay, Benny. I understand."

"When the ambulance came and they were loaded in they was both breathin', Nick. I swear. Your old man was breathin'."

"I believe you, Benny."

He put his elbows on his knees, and his head in his hands.

"Benny, I have to go and call my brother and my sister," I said. "Will you be okay?"

"Yeah, yeah, I'll be okay."

"Okay," I said. "I'll be right back."

I got up and walked to the pay phones. I dialed my brother's church first.

"Nick?" Vinnie said. "What're you doing? I'm supposed to be hearing confessions."

"It's Dad, Father Vinnie," I said. "He was havin' lunch with the Barracuda and somebody shot them."

"What?"

"They're in emergency at Victory Memorial Hospital," I said. "Better get over here fast, Vinnie. He needs his oldest son, and his priest."

"Damn it . . . have you called Maria?"

"No, I was gonna do that next—"

"I'll go and get her, and bring her with me," Vinnie said. "We'll be there as soon as we can."

"Okay, Vin."

"Nick . . . how is he?"

"Alive, Vinnie," I said, "they're both alive . . . so far."

"See you soon."

We hung up, and I went back out to sit with Benny.

Ten

VINNIE AND MARIA GOT THERE WITHIN HALF-AN-HOUR. BENNY AND I both stood when they came in, but Benny held back as I went to greet them. I had to duck, bob and weave to keep from being flattened in the crowded E.R.

"Nicky!" my sister said, coming into my arms and crying.

"How are they?" Vinnie asked.

"Still no word," I said. "Vinnie, I hate to ask, but . . ."

"What?"

"You've got your collar on."

He knew what I meant immediately.

"I'll go and see what I can find out."

I'd tried to get my older brother to use his white collar before to get us better seats at a game, or a restaurant, but he always refused. This time was totally different.

He went to the front desk and spoke with the same nurse, then came back to us.

"They're gonna let me in, just in case one of them needs last rites."

"Oh, Vinnie . . ." my sister sobbed.

"They're still working on them, Maria," Vinnie said. "I'll just go and find out how bad they are."

"Go ahead," I said, still holding Maria. "Hurry, Vin."

He went and I took Maria to the chair between me and Benny, which she could use because she was so small.

She asked me what happened and I told her while Benny sat there looking miserable and guilty.

A few minutes later, when she went to the ladies room, I said to Benny, "What's goin' on, Benny?"

"Whastaya mean?"

"There's no soldiers here," I said. "I thought when a Don got hit—even a retired Don--the soldiers turned out to protect him."

"I ain't called anybody," he admitted.

"Why not?"

"Because I don't know who to trust," Benny said, keeping his voice low. "I only called you Nicky, 'cause I trust you. You and me, we'll keep 'im safe."

I had grabbed my thirty-eight out of the safe in my office floor before heading for the hospital. After all, Benny had just told me that both my father and godfather had been shot. And I knew Benny was heeled. He always was.

"What about the cops?" I asked. "Why aren't they here?"

"I didn't call for 'em," he said. "I just called for an ambulance."

"Well, they'll be here, as soon as the hospital reports they have two gunshot wounds here."

As if on cue flashing lights reflected from outside, and when the automatic doors opened, two uniformed cops came walking in.

"I'll take this," I said to Benny, and rose to meet them.

The cops were from the Sixty-Eighth Precinct in Bay Ridge, where the hospital was located. Before long we also had detectives from the Sixty-Eighth and then detectives from the Sixty-First. The Sixty-First were representing Sheepshead Bay, where the shooting took place.

I had to talk to all of them, while trying to keep them away from Benny. He was wound up so tight there was no telling what he'd say or do when pressed about why he hadn't called the cops immediately. If they searched him and found his gun they might use it as an excuse to haul him in.

Meanwhile, I had to keep one eye on Maria, and another one out for Vinnie. I was running out of eyes.

Eventually, we were all just waiting for a doctor to come out and tell us what was going on.

Finally, one did.

The detectives charged him immediately, but he brushed them off and came to me.

"Are you Mr. Delvecchio's son?" he asked. He had on a name tag that said Doctor Ramirez. He was in his forties, gray hair and mustache, and just the slightest Spanish accent.

"I am."

"And I'm his daughter," Maria said, rushing up to my side. "How is he?"

"We're still working on him," he said, "but he has a very rare blood type. We're getting some now from Father Vincent, but we're going to need more."

"We're ready," Maria said.

Ramirez looked at her.

"I think we'll be able to get what we need from your two brothers."

"But—"

"Gimme a minute, Doc."

He nodded. I took Maria by the shoulders and pulled her away to where nobody would be able to hear us. It wasn't easy, but there was one corner we were able to use.

"Maria, I need you to stay and look after Benny," I said.

"But Nick—"

"If we leave him alone with these cops he's gonna end up in trouble. I need him out of jail if I'm gonna find out who shot Pop."

"Nicky, you're not gonna—"

"Hell, yeah, I am," I said. "You don't think I'm gonna leave this to the cops, do you? Come on, Maria. I need you now."

"All right," she said, "all right." She took two fists full of my shirt. "But you let me know if something happens!"

"I will. I swear."

I walked over to Ramirez and said, "Let's go, Doc."

Eleven

HE TOOK ME THROUGH A SET OF DOUBLE DOORS, INTO THE BACK, TO WHERE Vinnie was lying down on a gurney with a tube in his arm. I looked around for the Don, and for my Pop.

"Where are they?" I asked.

"We have them in operating rooms upstairs," Ramirez said. "We'll take your blood down here."

"Okay."

"But first I have to test and make sure you have the same type."

"I'm his son," I said.

"Do you know your blood type? Or his?"

I had to admit I didn't.

"It's just a formality," he said. "I'll check for your type, and then we'll pump you dry."

"What?"

"Just kidding. Lie down over here."

I laid down on a table next to Vinnie. There was a curtain between us, but it was open. The doctor found a good vein in my arm, swabbed me and took a vial of blood.

"I'll be right back."

I turned my head to look at Vinnie.

"Did you see them?" I asked.

"Yeah, they took me upstairs."

"How are they?"

"Still alive."

"Vinnie," I asked, "do you have that thing . . ."

"What thing?"

"You know," I said, "that purple scarf thing you put around your neck when you give last rites. Do you have it with you?"

"My stole?"

"Yeah, that thing."

"Yes, Nick," he said, "I always have it with me. It's folded up in my jacket pocket."

"Okay," I said. "I just wanted to make sure."

A nurse came and removed the tube from his arm. She told Vinnie to stay there a while.

Doctor Ramirez reappeared after about ten minutes—I don't remember how long exactly—and looked at both of us.

"Father, perhaps you should come upstairs with me."

"What's wrong?" I asked.

Vinnie sat up, and I did, too. I helped him off his table.

"What is it?" Vinnie asked.

"I think you should come up," Ramirez said, again.

"Is he—" I started to ask.

"Not yet," the doctor said, "but soon."

"All right," Vinnie said.

"I'm comin', too," I said.

"Nick—"

"You might get lightheaded, Vin," I said. "I'm comin'."

Vinnie looked at the doctor.

"All right," he said, "but please hurry."

They took us up in an elevator to the floor where the operating room was. We were quiet on the ride up. I felt cold, inside. I hadn't come close to shedding a tear yet, maybe because I'd been taking care of Benny, and then Maria. Now, knowing that my father might be dead by the time we got to the right floor, I still felt calm. Maybe I'd been ready to hear the news from the moment I'd gotten there.

When we entered the operating room there were people standing around in blue scrubs, many of them soaked through with sweat, covered with blood.

Another doctor approached us, took off his mask.

"I'm sorry," he said. "We did all we could, there was just too much damage. The arteries leading to his heart were shredded. We tried to take some from his leg to graft, but we didn't have enough time . . ."

Vinnie took his stole from his pocket and put it around his neck. We both approached the operating table, he on Pop's right and me on the left. Pop's face looked gray, even though he had probably only died in the last few minutes. He was covered to the neck with a bloody sheet.

Vinnie made the sign of the cross, started to speak, giving him last rites, but I wasn't listening. I reached between the sheets to take my father's hand and hold it tightly.

"I'm sorry, Pop," I said. "I'm so sorry."

Twelve

THEY COVERED MY FATHER'S FACE WITH A SHEET AND WE LEFT THE ROOM. I was numb, and there were still no tears. I'd seen lots of death before, but what was wrong with me? This was my Pop.

I turned to a doctor and asked, "Where's Don—where's Mr. Barracondi?"

"In the next operating room," the doctor said. "His wounds are serious, but I believe we're going to be able to save him."

"Can we see him?" I asked.

"I'm sorry," the doctor said, "I can't—"

"Mr. Barracondi is my brother's godfather, Doctor," Vinnie said. "Do you know what that means in an Italian family?"

I don't know which meaning the doctor was thinking of but he said, "Well, all right. But just for a moment."

We walked to the door of the next room. The doctor went in first, me behind him. Somebody tied a mask around my mouth from behind, and then they let me approach the table.

The old man's blue eyes looked as bright as ever as he saw me. There was an oxygen mask over his face, which was pale, but not gray. He reached a heavily veined hand out to me and I took it. His grip was weak. There were tubes in his arm.

He started to say something but the mask muffled the sound.

Knowing him, I was sure he was trying to ask about my father. It was better that he didn't know yet.

I released his hand and allowed the doctor to steer me out of the room.

"How is he?" I asked. "Why aren't they workin' on him?"

"He needs more surgery," the doctor said. "We're waiting for him to stabilize, first. It will be some time before we're finished with him."

"I see."

Doctor Ramirez said, "I'll take you both back down."

"Are you sure you won't need me—" Vinnie started to ask.

"No," the other doctor said. "I think we've got this one, Father."

Ramirez took Vinnie and me back down. On the way in the elevator Vinnie took off the stole, folded it lovingly and put it back in his pocket. We didn't speak. One of us was going to have to tell Maria that Pop was dead.

When we reentered the emergency room it was full of people. There were still uniformed cops, but now there were two sergeants and a lieutenant. The detectives from both squads were still there, too.

Maria was sitting next to Benny, holding his big hands in hers. When they saw us they both got to their feet.

"Mr. Delvecchio—" the lieutenant said.

"Lieutenant," my brother said, "in a minute, please."

"Father, I understand what's going on, but we need to talk—"

"Talk to me, then," Vinnie said. "My brother has to give some bad news to our sister."

I nodded to Vinnie and went to talk to Benny and Maria.

"Nick?" she said, studying my face.

"I'm so sorry, Maria," I said. "He's gone."

Her eyes overflowed with tears and as they streamed down her face her mouth opened, but no sound came out. I grabbed her and pulled her to me so that when she did scream it would be muffled by my chest.

"I'm sorry, Nick," Benny said, putting a big hand on my shoulder.

"Benny," I said, "the Don's gonna be okay."

His eyes went wide.

"Can I see 'im? I should be with him."

"It's gonna be a while," I said. "He still needs some more surgery."

"But Nick, I gotta—"

"Benny," I said, "there are probably gonna be a lot of cops up there soon. Don't do anything silly, okay? It won't do the Don any good for you to get yourself tossed in jail."

"Yeah," he said, "yeah, okay, Nick. Geez, I'm really sorry about your dad. He was a good guy."

Rubbing my sister's back while she sobbed I said, "Yeah, he was a good guy."

Vinnie came over. "Nick, I think you ought to talk to the police. That's more your department."

"Yeah, okay," I said. I handed Maria over to him and turned to talk to the police.

Thirteen

I ENDED UP IN A SMALL ROOM WITH THE DETECTIVES FROM THE SIX-ONE, since that's where the shooting took place.

They were a mismatched pair, the older on—Detective Blaine—in his early fifties with a receding hairline and granite jaw. His partner, Detective Hart, was in his thirties, with a weak jaw that worked furiously on a piece of gum.

The room was an examining room, filled mostly with Blaine's bulk. Luckily, Hart and I together barely took up the same amount of space as he did.

"We've already questioned your friend, Benny," Blaine said.

"You did?" That was news to me.

"He told us what happened," Hart said.

"Then what do you need me for?" I asked. "I just lost my father. I've got things to do."

"We understand," Blaine said. "We'll only keep you a few minutes."

"Okay, whatever," I said.

"Did you talk to Nick Barracuda when you were upstairs?" Blaine asked.

"That's what you want to know?"

"We figure Barracuda maybe told you who the shooters were."

"First of all his name is Mr. Barracondi," I said. "Have a little respect. The man's lying upstairs with holes in him."

"You're pretty defensive of a man who probably got your father killed," Hart said. "The shooters must've been after him, and your old man got in the way."

"That means the shooters are at fault, not the D—not my godfather."

"Godfather," Blaine said. "That's rich."

"He happens to *be* my godfather," I said.

"Look," Blaine said, "we all know who Nicky Barracuda is, Delvecchio. Somebody tried to take out the Don, and got your father at the same time. Seems to me you'd be wantin' to help us find out who it was."

"What did the Barracuda say to you upstairs?" Hart asked.

"Nothin'," I said. "He can't talk, yet. He still needs some more surgery."

"Look," Blaine said, "we're just doing the preliminary on this. Your dad died, that means Brooklyn South Homicide is gonna get this case. So if you don't help us, you'll have to help them."

"Detective," I said, "believe me, there's nothin' I want more than to find out who did this."

"Don't think you're gonna be able to go lone wolf on this, Delvecchio," Blaine said. "This was a Mafia hit. You can't take them on alone, no matter how far they've fallen in the past few years."

Since John Gotti, supposedly the Last Don, was sentenced to life in prison in 1992 the Mafia had fallen on hard times. They were no longer the crime power they had once been. Other so called "mafias" had popped up, most notably the Russians.

"Maybe it wasn't the Italian Mafia who did this," I said.

"You mean the Russians?"

"Or the South Americans. Or the Koreans," I said. "Who knows?"

"Well," Blaine said, closing his notebook, "let Homicide worry about it. They'll question Barracuda when he's ready to talk."

"Well it ain't gonna be tonight," I said. "Can I go? I've got arrangements to make."

"Sure, go ahead," Blaine said. "You're not bein' any help to us. If we patted you and your buddy down would we find you both heeled?"

"I don't know," I said. "Would you?"

Hart stood up but Blaine put his hands on his partner's chest.

"I'm givin' you a pass, Delvecchio, because your dad was killed tonight. Don't count on the same pass from Homicide. Those guys are a little more hard ass than I am."

"I'll keep that in mind," I said, then as an afterthought said, "Thanks."

I wasn't being any help to them because I couldn't be. I didn't know squat. The Don hadn't told me anything, and Benny didn't know anything helpful. Once I could talk to the Don, and ask some questions around Sheepshead Bay, maybe I'd get some answers.

But right at that moment all I could really do was try to deal with the death of my father.

Fourteen

HOURS LATER IT WAS JUST US IN THE EMERGENCY ROOM. ME, VINNIE, MARIA and Benny. There was nothing else the police could do until the Don was able to talk. There was one cop upstairs, waiting to take a statement.

Other emergencies had come in, been taken care of, and either admitted or released. There were still a few people sitting and either waiting to be seen, or waiting for someone being treated. One person was cradling an arm, another was holding a handkerchief to his nose. Even though the E.R. had been crowded for a while, it had been a relatively slow night for Victory Memorial's emergency room. And for Brooklyn. Odd.

An odd night, all around.

"Can we take him home?" Maria asked.

"What?"

"Dad," she said. "Can we take him home?"

"I doubt it," I said. "They'll want an autopsy."

"Autopsy? What for? He was shot."

"Mandatory for homicides," I said.

"What about the Don?" Benny asked. "Are they gonna let me go up and see him?"

"Probably when they put him in a room."

"Private room," Benny said. "It has to be a private room."

"We can arrange that."

Father Vinnie was quiet, head bowed. I thought he was praying.

"Sir?"

I looked up. It was the reception nurse—a different one from before. I hadn't seen her or spoken to her, yet. This one was older, gray-haired, very businesslike.

"Yes?"

"I'm sorry, but I need to have you fill out some papers."

"Papers?"

"Yes, for billing?"

"Billing?" Maria asked, appalled. "You want to talk to us about billing . . . now?"

"I'm sorry," the woman said, "but it's my job."

"Listen, lady—"

"Nick," Benny said. "I'll take care of it. The Don would want to take care of it."

"Benny—"

"I got it," Benny said. He stood up, towering over the woman, who stared up at him in awe. "Come on, dear."

He took her elbow and led her back to her desk. Another oddity. Benny, being gentle, and even charming.

"The Church has medical insurance," Vinnie said.

"Uncle Dom will take care of it," I said.

"I haven't heard you call him that in a long time," Maria said.

"I know."

The double doors opened and Doctor Ramirez came out. I stood up and went to meet him.

"Can we talk?" he asked.

"Sure."

He looked past me at Maria and Father Vinnie, and said, "Away from the others."

"Anything you want to say to me you can say in front of my brother and sister."

"I think maybe I'll leave it up to you, if you want to tell them later," he said.

I studied his face for a few moments, not really getting anything from him. I turned and said, "I'll be right back."

I followed him through the double doors and into a treatment room.

"What's goin' on, Doc?"

"Your blood."

"What about it."

"When I took the sample I checked it for compatibility."

"Yeah, so?" I stared at him. "Oh great, you're gonna tell me you found something in my blood. Am I sick?"

"No, no," he said, "you're not sick. But I did find something."

"What?"

"I gave it a lot of thought before deciding to tell you," he said.

"Tell me what, Doc?"

"Well . . . your blood type."

"Yeah?"

"It, uh, doesn't match."

"Match what?"

"Your father's blood type—you weren't a match. We would not have been able to use your blood on him, just your—just Father Vincent's."

"Doc," I said, "you're gonna have to spit this out in plain English for me."

"Well," he said, "simply put . . . your father is—was—not your father."

Fifteen

WAS IT ODD THAT OF EVERYTHING THAT HAD HAPPENED THAT NIGHT, this was what hit me the hardest? I felt like I'd been hit square in the belly. I couldn't take a breath.

"Mr. Delvecchio?" Doctor Ramirez said. "Are you all right?"

I couldn't answer.

"Come over here, sit down." He led me to a chair and lowered me into it.

I looked up at him and said, "Wha—what?"

"I'm sorry," the doctor said. "Obviously, you didn't know you were . . . adopted? Some parents don't ever tell the child . . ."

"Adopted?" I said.

"That's the only explanation I can think of."

Of course, given the business I was in, I could think of another possibility.

"Your blood type is O positive. It's the most common type. Your father was B positive, not the rarest, but still rare."

"And . . . my brother?"

"Father Vincent is also B positive. Do you know what your mother's blood type was?"

"N-no." If I didn't know mine before that night, how would I know my mother's?

"I'm sorry . . ."

I stared at the floor, my mind racing. I didn't like where it was going, though, so I tried to shake it off.

"Can I . . . get you anything?" he asked.

"No," I said, "no, I'm fine. How's the Don—how's my godfather?"

"He resting easy," Ramirez said. "We moved him to Critical Care."

"Can we go up?"

"Sure," Ramirez said, "it's the eighth floor, but there's a policeman up there."

"I'll talk to him," I said. "Thanks, Doctor."

"Mr. Delvecchio," he said, "you had more than one shock tonight. Perhaps you should go home, get some rest."

"I will, Doctor," I said, "soon."

"I . . . I hope I did the right thing in telling you," he said, with concern.

"You did, Doctor," I assured him, "you did."

"Everything okay?" Father Vinnie asked when I returned to the emergency waiting room. People were moving around us very quickly.

"Yeah, what's happening?"

"Some kind of accident. They're bringing in a lot of casualties."

"Then we better get out of here."

Benny came over.

"What's going on, Nick?"

"The Don is in Critical Care," I said. "We can go up. When we get there I'll have to talk to the police officer."

"Let's go!" Benny said.

"Get Maria, Benny."

He went to where she was sitting and helped her to her feet.

"Is everything okay, Nick?"

"Nothing's okay, Vinnie."

"No, of course not. I know that. I just meant . . . with you. Are you all right?"

"I don't think I'll know until I get home," I said. "All of this has to . . . process."

"I don't think any of us should be alone tonight, Nick. We can all go to Maria's."

"Or Pop's," I said.

We all had keys to my father's house. After all, we used to live there.

"Let's go," Benny said, with Maria looking on.

●

WHEN WE got out of the elevator we came face-to-face with the police officer, a young guy with "Deaver" on his chest.

"Officer Deaver."

"Who are you people?"

"Delvecchio," I said. "I'm Nick, this is Maria, and . . . Father Vincent."

"Oh, hello, Father," Deaver said.

Good, I thought, a Catholic.

"And this is Benny. We'd like to see Mr. Barracondi."

"Are you family?"

"Yes," I said. "He's our uncle. Our father was killed in the attack on both of them."

"I'm supposed to take a statement when he comes to," the cop said.

"No problem," I said. "We just want to see him, and one of us will be staying all night."

"I'll have to okay that with my boss."

"Talk to Detective Blaine, Six-One Squad."

"Six-One?" He looked confused. "But we're in the Six-Eight."

"Talk to Dr. Ramirez," Vinnie said.

"Dr. Ramirez?"

Another elevator opened and Ramirez stepped out.

"I'm sorry," he said to me. "I was delayed."

"Hey, Doc, these folks wanna see Mr. Barracondi—"

"Yes, yes, it's all right," the doctor said. "They won't stay long."

"They say one of them will be staying all night."

Ramirez frowned.

"Is that right?"

"Vinnie," I said, "take Benny and Maria in to see . . . Uncle Dom."

"Oh, I'm afraid that won't be—" Ramirez started, but I cut him off.

"Doctor, do you know who you have in there?"

"Uh, Mr. Barracondi? Your uncle."

"Let me tell you a little about Dominick Barracondi," I said.

Sixteen

WHEN I ENTERED THE ROOM, VINNIE TURNED TO LOOK AT ME.

"All right?" he asked.

"The doctor now knows who he has here," I said. "He said 'oh, that Godfather.' He understands the need for Benny to stay. He also thinks that a bunch of mafia foot soldiers are gonna storm the hospital at any moment."

"Did he see *The Godfather*?" Vinnie asked.

"Yeah, he did," I said. "He also saw *Casino* this year. But I assured him that Uncle Dom is not Marlon Brando and Benny's not Al Pacino and there are no Joe Pesci's on the way. But I also convinced him that there was a need for Benny to stay, even if it was Benny's need."

"I wouldn't want to be the one to tell Benny he couldn't stay," Vinnie said.

"Me, neither," I said, "and the doctor doesn't want to be that man, either."

"What about the cop?"

"I think the doctor convinced him for us," I said. "Of course, when the detectives come back in the morning that'll change, but until then . . ."

"I talked to Maria about all of us going back to Pop's, and she agreed. She doesn't want to be alone tonight."

"Okay."

"There's somethin' else on your mind, isn't there, Nick?"

"Yeah, there is, Vin," I said, "but we'll talk about it later. I've got to talk to Benny. Why don't you take Maria out into the hall?"

"Okay."

Vinnie steered Maria out and I went to stand next to Benny.

"Ben."

"He don't look too good, Nicky," he said.

"The doctor says he'll be fine, barring complications."

"Don't they always say that?"

"Yeah," I said, "it kinda covers them. Look, you can stay tonight."

"Damn right, I'm stayin'!"

"No, I mean I got you permission," I said. "Don't get into it with the cop outside. If the Don wakes up it's his job to write down whatever he says. You gotta let him, you hear?"

"I hear ya, Nick."

"And if the detectives come back early and kick you out, don't argue," I said. "It won't do the Don any good for you to get yourself tossed in jail. Got it?"

"I got it," he said, "but what do I do then? If they kick me out?"

"Go back downstairs and wait for me," I said. "I'll be back in the morning."

"Okay."

"I'll bring you some breakfast."

"Thanks, Nick. Hey, about your dad—"

"It's okay, Benny," I said. "I know, okay?"

"Sure."

"I'll see you in the morning," I said. "And look, don't pull that gun unless you absolutely have to, okay?"

"I ain't stupid, Nick."

"I know that, Benny," I said. "Believe me, I know it."

I slapped him on his broad back, took one more look down at the Don—who was still hooked up to tubes and monitors—and then went out to grieve with my brother and sister.

Or whoever they were.

Seventeen

My Dad's house—the house I grew up in—was in Bensonhurst on Ovington Avenue, between Fourteenth and Fifteenth Streets. The thing I really enjoyed about my childhood—apart from my mother's cooking—was that we were walking distance from pizza, bagels and Chinese food.

As we entered the house Maria went into mother mode, which was good for her.

"I'll make coffee."

She went into the kitchen with the bag of bagels we had stopped to pick up around the corner at the 24-hour shop.

Vinnie and I stood for a moment in the hall. I knew we were both thinking the same thing: What do we do now?

Only I was wrong. That wasn't what Vinnie was thinking.

"What's wrong, Nick?"

"What do you mean?"

"Something happened tonight. Something other than Pop and Uncle Dom being shot. What is it?"

I peered down the hall to the kitchen, where Maria was keeping herself busy.

"Come into the living room."

He followed me there. I turned to him and kept my voice down.

"Did you know what your blood type was when they asked you?"

"Not really," Vinnie said. "I guess I should have but—"

"Never mind," I said. "Here's my point. The doctor told me my blood was the wrong type for Pop."

"Well," Vinnie said, "they had mine, and given what happened I guess it really didn't matter—"

"You don't understand," I said. "The doctor said there's no way I could be related to Pop."

"What?" Vinnie looked puzzled.

"We don't have the same father, Vin."

He stared at me with his mouth open, then said, "That can't be."

"That's what I said."

"It's gotta be a mistake, Nick."

"The doctor said he double-checked it."

Vinnie sat down heavily on the sofa. Maria startled the hell out of both of us by appearing and asking, "You guys want the bagels in here."

"Yeah, that's good," I said.

She nodded and went back to the kitchen.

I sat down on the sofa with Vinnie.

"What does this mean, Nick?"

"The doctor thought it meant I was adopted."

"Adopted? Why would you be adopted? Mom and Pop had Joe, then me. Why adopt you, and then have Maria?"

"Didn't make sense to me, either."

"Then what's the explanation?"

I hesitated, then said, "You won't like it."

"What?"

I shrugged. "Maybe Pop didn't know."

Vinnie stared at me for a few moments until the meaning of what I was suggesting set in.

"Oh, no . . . Mom?"

I shrugged again. "The doctor's got no reason to lie, Vin."

"I know, but . . . Mom? And somebody else?"

"I know," I said.

"I don't believe it," Vinnie said.

"Don't believe what?" Maria asked. She entered the room carrying a tray with coffee cups and a platter of bagels and butter.

I looked at Vinnie, who just stared back at me. How would Maria react to this after everything that had happened that night?

She walked to the coffee table and put the tray down on it.

"The coffee will be ready soon," she said. "What's goin' on? You don't believe what, Vinnie?"

Maria hadn't had an easy time of it for the past few years. She had gotten divorced, was on a hijacked plane, and had to live through—as we all did—the time that Father Vinnie was suspected of having an affair with a parishioner, and murder.

Now this. Pop was dead, and apparently, he wasn't my real father.

"Nick? Vinnie? What's goin' on?"

"Sit down, Maria."

She sat in one of the armchairs, staring at both of us warily.

"You guys are scarin' me," she said. "What could be as bad, or worse, than what happened to Pop?"

"Well," I said, "Apparently—the doctors were taking blood from Vinnie, and wanted to take some from me, except . . ."

"Except what?"

"I didn't match."

"Can that be?" she asked. "How could that be?"

"That's what we were wondering," Vinnie said.

"And . . . what's that mean?"

"Well . . ." I said. "According to the doctor . . . Pop wasn't my real father."

She stared at me for a few seconds, then buried her face in her hands and started crying.

Eighteen

VINNIE WENT TO THE KITCHEN TO GET THE COFFEE. MARIA HAD HAD ENOUGH. The news I'd just given her was the last straw, and she just dissolved. I crouched next to her while Vinnie went to the kitchen.

"Take it easy, Maria . . ." I said.

"I can't take it, Nick," she said. "Pop's dead, and now you're tryin' to tell me you're not . . . not my brother, anymore?"

"I'm always gonna be your brother," I assured her. "That's not gonna change."

"But . . . but what's this mean?"

"That's what Vinnie and I were tryin' to figure out."

I didn't tell her about the possibilities we'd come up with. No point in upsetting her even more.

Vinnie came in with the coffee pot, filled all our cups, and we took the time to butter our bagels and take bites. Never let it be said that an Italian family allowed adversity to effect its appetite.

Vinnie and I started to turn the subject away from the blood types. We talked about who would do what—make calls to family, talk to the funeral home, talk to the cops—me, of course—and so on.

"What about Uncle Dom?" Maria asked. "Who's gonna take care of him?"

"I guess that'll be Benny," I said.

"Benny?" Maria asked. "And who's gonna take care of *him*?"

We finished our bagels and coffee and I said to Vinnie, "How about a beer?"

He gave me a wry look and said, "I'm sure Pop has some in the refrigerator."

"I'll take this tray back into the kitchen," Maria said, "and get three beers."

"Three?"

"Sure," she said. "Why can't I have a beer with my . . . brothers?" She looked right at me when she said it, defiantly, then took the tray and left the room.

"She's gonna be okay," Vinnie said.

"Until the funeral."

"We just have to let her take care of us," Vinnie said. "That'll keep her busy."

"Yeah," I said, "us, and maybe Benny."

"That's a good idea," he said. "Make her feel really needed."

"I'll talk to Benny later."

"He'll be at the hospital."

"I know," I said. "He won't go home. I should bring him some fresh clothes."

"How will you know his size?" Vinnie asked.

"He's been the same size since high school," I said, holding my hands as far apart as I could. "Size Benny."

Vinnie laughed.

"He wasn't at the reunion, was he?"

"No," I said. "Man, the reunion, that seems years away, now."

And so did Mary Ann's death, and agreeing to look into it. Now I had my own death in the family to look into.

Maria came back with three bottles of Rolling Rock, the caps already removed.

"What are you gonna do, Nick?" she asked.

"Whataya mean?"

"I know you," she said, "and Father Vinnie knows you."

"She's right," Vinnie said. "We know you're not gonna take this laying down. You're not about to sit back and let the police handle this."

"What are your plans?" Maria asked.

"What makes you think I have any plans, yet?"

"Like she said, Nicky," Vinnie said. "We know you."

I took a swig from the cold green bottle in my hand and looked at both of them.

"Okay," I said. "First I have to go back to the hospital, talk to Benny and to the Don. After that I'm gonna have to talk to the Homicide dicks. Weinstock is still assigned there. We get along."

"Then what?" Maria asked. "Will they work with you?"

"Oh, no," I said, "they'll warn me off. Threaten me. Blah-blah-blah."

"But you said you got along with them," Maria said.

"That doesn't mean they'll want me in their business."

"But . . . this is our business. Family business."

"You're right, Maria, it is."

"I don't know . . ." Vinnie said.

Maria and I both looked at him.

"Pop's dead, Vinnie," I said. "That makes it our business."

"But this is what the police do."

"Don't forget," I told him, "it's what I do, too."

He took a sip of his beer and looked dubious.

"Okay," he said, "what else?"

"I'll have to go to Sheepshead Bay and ask questions," I said. "See if anyone saw anything."

"Can I come and help?" Maria asked.

"Oh," I said, "oh, no, Maria. You and Vinnie will have to stay out of it."

"But . . . you just said it's family business."

"Yeah, but I'll handle it," I said. "We're dealing with people with guns, who aren't afraid to use them. You and Vinnie have to just stay out of it. Besides, it'll be up to the two of you to plan Pop's funeral."

I looked at Vinnie and jerked my head, hoping he'd get the message and leave me alone with Maria.

"Be right back," he said. putting down his beer bottle. "Stuff goes right through me."

As he left the room I moved closer to Maria.

"Listen," I said, "I'm gonna need your help, after all."

"Good," she said. "What can I do?"

"I need you to take care of Vinnie," I said.

"But . . . he's a priest."

"I know," I said. "That means everyone will expect him to take care of everything. And like you said about Benny, who'll take care of Vinnie? He's gonna need you, Maria."

"Okay, yeah," she said. "I understand."

"You and Vinnie will have to notify the rest of the family, such as they are."

"Oh," she said, "right. uncles, aunts, cousins . . ."

There were a lot of them, but we hadn't seen them in some time. Still, they deserved to know.

"And then there's Benny," I continued, "like you said, he'll need somebody to talk to."

"But he has you."

"That's true, but he may need you, too."

"I can't imagine Benny needing a woman," she said, "I mean, other than . . . you know . . ."

"I know." Most of Benny's relationships with women had been professional. When he needed companionship, he called a whore.

"Isn't Benny gonna want to help you investigate?" she asked.

"I'm sure he will, and I'll let him," I said. "I'm gonna need his contacts to get me to the other families."

We were talking about different family, now.

"God," she said, shaking her head, "this is gonna get all Mario Puzo on us, isn't it?"

I hugged her and said, "I'm afraid it is."

Nineteen

I DECIDED TO GO HOME TO GET MYSELF READY TO LOOK INTO THE SHOOTING. Vinnie and Maria were going to spend the rest of the day at my father's house, calling family. I walked past my office door to enter through the other one. As I walked in, my foot encountered something on the floor. A 3x5 envelope. I picked it up and unfolded the note inside.

"Where have you been?" it asked. Signed SAM.

Jesus, I'd forgotten to tell Sam what happened with my dad and the Don. Normally I would have banged on her door when something unusual happened. She was pretty much the only person I talked to other than my brother the Father. I didn't have drinking buddies.

She was going to be pissed!

I decided to get it over with. I went across the hall and knocked on her door. It was late afternoon, but I knew she'd be up.

"There you are!" she said, as she opened her door. She had her straw colored hair pulled back in a ponytail, which she only did when she was working. She was wearing a tank top that was stretched tight across her breasts, and short shorts. She never went out on the street like that, but in the privacy of her own home I was surprised she didn't go naked most of the time. Actually, I was glad she didn't. I'd be across the hall thinking about it all the time.

"Where have you been? I've been waitin' for you."

"Come across the hall," I said, "and I'll tell you."

She stared at my face. "Nick? What happened?"

She followed me into my apartment, closed the door behind her, then turned, a serious look on her face.

"Nick?"

"My dad's dead."

"What?"

"He was shot to death yesterday."

"Omigod!"

She grabbed me immediately and pulled me close. I buried my face in her neck and almost cried. I breathed her in, comforted by her scent, and her touch.

"I'm so sorry!" she said, rubbing my back.

We stood like that for a while, then stepped apart with no hint of awkwardness. There was always sexual tension between us, but at the end of the day we were friends.

"God, you've been up all night, haven't you?" she asked.

"Yeah, I have. I just came from my father's house, left Vinnie and Maria there."

"Nick, what happened?"

"Sit down, Sam," I said. "I just need to get some coffee first."

"I'll make it" she said. "You sit down and relax, because if I know you, you've got all sorts of reasons why you shouldn't go right to bed now and get a few hours' sleep."

Yeah, she knew me.

I sat on the sofa and Sam had to wake me up to hand me a mug of coffee.

"How long was I asleep?"

"Five minutes."

She sat next to me on the sofa, also holding a mug of coffee.

"Okay," she said, "tell me."

I told her everything that had happened, saving the part about the blood tests. As far as I was concerned that was completely separate from the shooting, and would have to spend some time on the back burner.

"Oh, my God," she said. "What can you do about it, Nick. You've got to leave this to the police."

"The police can't go where I can go, Sam," I said. "They don't know the people I know."

"That may be, but this is the Mafia, Nick."

"Sam, they're not as scary as they make out in the movies," I said, then added to myself, well, not anymore.

"Scary enough to shoot down two men in broad daylight," she said. "Besides, isn't it obvious who did it? And who they were after?"

"Whoever did it," I said, "and whoever they were after, they still managed to kill my dad. I'm not gonna walk away from that."

"That's your ego talking, Nick."

"Maybe," I said. "Maybe it is." I put the coffee mug down and rubbed my face vigorously with both hands.

"I'm gonna take a shower, see if that wakes me up," I said.

"Sure," she said. "I'll wait here."

I went into the bathroom, got undressed and under the shower. I meant for it to be quick, because to tell you the truth, I hate showers.

Twenty

"JESUS," SAM SAID, WHEN I CAME WALKING OUT DRESSED IN SWEATS, "were you in there two minutes?"

"Just long enough."

"If your hair wasn't wet . . ."

"You want a beer?" I asked.

"Sure."

I went to the kitchen, came back with two bottles of Brooklyn Brown Ale for me and an India Pale Ale for her. Both came from the Brooklyn Brewery.

"What else is going on, Nick?"

"Whataya mean?"

"I mean we've been neighbors and friends for a few years," she said. "I know when something's bothering you."

"You don't think what I've told you is enough?"

"It's plenty," she said, "but there's more, isn't there?"

I sipped my beer and asked, "What are you, a witch?"

"When it comes to you, yeah."

"Okay," I said, "sit down for this one."

We sat, and I told her about the blood tests.

"And you believe this?" she asked.

"What's not to believe?" I asked. "What reason would the doctor have to lie? He double-checked the results."

"I still think you should get a second opinion," she said.

"Yeah, well, you're probably right," I said, "but I don't think it's as important as finding out who killed him."

"You know," she said, "he's the man who raised you. No matter what happens, he was your father."

"Yeah," I said, "but if it's true, what does it say about my mother?"

She stared at me for a minute, then said, "Oh."

"Yeah, right."

"Have you told your brother and sister?"

"I told them."

"How'd they take it?"

"Vinnie was okay," I said. "Maria didn't take it well, but she's all right. I've given her some things to keep her busy."

"That's good."

"She and Vinnie are notifying the rest of the family."

"Are there a lot?"

"It's an Italian family," I said. "We have so many relatives we think it's okay not to be talking to half of them. But they'll all have to be notified."

"What about . . . Don Barracondi?"

"Benny will notify whoever needs to be."

"I'm not up on my Mafia etiquette," she said. "He's retired, right? So does this start some kind of war?"

"I'm not sure," I said. "I'm sure along the way someone will tell me, though."

"Isn't this gonna be dangerous?" she asked. "I mean, getting involved in their business."

"This is my family business, Sam," I said. "If anyone will understand that, they will."

"I guess so."

I finished my beer and asked, "Want another one?"

"No," she said. "In fact, I'll take this one with me back to my apartment. I've still got three chapters to write."

"I'm sorry I interrupted your work," I said.

"Don't be dumb," she said. "I wish you'd told me yesterday. I could've been at the hospital with you."

And I knew she would have been, too.

I walked her to the door and she kissed me on the cheek.

"Let me know if I can do anything," she said. "You know, help with the funeral, or at the house? Whatever."

"I will, Sam," I said. "Thanks."

I closed my door behind her, heard her door open and close. I got myself another beer and took it to my office.

The message machine was like a Christmas tree. There were several calls from Tony Mitts, a couple from Catherine, and one from Catherine's mother. There were still some old ones from a frantic Benny. I deleted them all. I was going to have to let them know I couldn't work on Mary Ann's death, not today.

I had other things to do.

I changed out of my sweats into jeans and a T-shirt and a pair of Rockports. Before leaving the office I put my gun back in the safe. I was going to be talking to the Homicide boys, probably in their office. Not a good idea to wear a gun into the police station.

But first, I had to go back to the hospital.

Twenty-One

I STOPPED OFF AT A DUANE READE AND A BIG MAN'S SHOP SO I COULD bring Benny a change of clothes and some other stuff he'd need to clean up—toothpaste, deodorant, a comb.

"Thanks, Nicky," he said, when I handed him the bags.

The cop outside the door didn't know me, but apparently had my name on a list, because he allowed me to enter the Don's room.

"How is he?"

"He opened his eyes a few times," Benny said. "I think he's just checkin' ta see if I'm here, because he just nods at me and goes back to sleep."

"Probably give you hell if you weren't here."

"Yeah, don't I know it."

"Doctor been in?"

"This mornin'," Benny said.

"What'd he say?"

"That I should go home and get some rest."

"He's probably right."

"You don't look like you got no rest."

"No, I didn't. Why don't you go into the bathroom and get changed."

"Yeah, okay."

"And I got some cologne, too," I called after him as he closed the door.

Alone with the Don I started down at him. He was pale as a ghost, but his chest seemed to be rising and falling evenly. The machine he was hooked up to was scrolling numbers and an uneven line kept beeping along.

I didn't realize I had my hand on the bed until I suddenly felt his hand close around my wrist. When I looked down he was staring up at me.

"Hey," I said, "you're okay."

He reached with a hand that looked more like a claw and dragged the oxygen mask away from his mouth.

"Vito," he said, "Vito . . ."

"He's dead, Godfather," I said. "Pop's dead."

He closed his eyes for a moment, then opened them, looked at me and said, *"Mea culpa . . . Mea culpa . . ."*

"No," I said, putting the oxygen mask back in place, "it's not your fault. It's the fault of whoever shot you, or whoever sent the shooters. Do you know who that was?"

He didn't answer.

"Just shake your head or nod, Godfather," I said. "Do you know who shot you and killed Pop?"

His eyes closed, and didn't reopen. But his chest was still moving up and down, so I knew he'd simply fallen asleep.

Benny came out of the bathroom with a clean shirt, combed hair and too much of the cologne I'd bought him splashed on. He was still wearing the same pants and shoes, of course. He obviously had his dirty laundry in the plastic Duane Reade bag.

"Did he wake up?"

"For a minute."

"What did he say?"

"He said Pop's name, and then he said it was his fault Pop's dead."

"It ain't his fault, Nicky."

"I know, Benny," I said. "I told him that."

"Good," Benny said. "It's important to him that you don't blame him."

"Have you and he talked?"

"Briefly," Benny said. "He ain't made much sense—not as much as he just made to you, anyway."

"Have the Homicide guys been here?"

"This mornin'," Benny said.

"Give you a hard time?"

"Yeah," Benny said. "They took my gun, Nick. I could use another one."

"I'll look into it," I said. "I left mine home for just that reason. I didn't want them taking it off me when I go see them."

"You gonna do that next?"

"Yeah, and then I'm goin' to Sheepshead Bay to have a look around."

Benny nodded, looked down at Nicky Barracuda.

"Benny," I said, "do we know who to trust?"

He looked at me sadly and said, "Not really, Nick. I mean, there's one or two guys I could tell you to depend on, but nobody who knows anything." He looked down at the Don again. "This coulda been ordered by anybody."

"Is there a power struggle goin' on?" I asked.

Benny shrugged. "The Don's retired, Nick."

"Come on, Benny," I said. "If there's a fight for power and he put his name behind somebody, it would mean somethin'."

"In the old days, maybe," Benny said. "Not so much now, Nick."

I frowned, looked down at the old man in the bed. If that was true, then who'd have reason to try and kill him?

Twenty-Two

THE OFFICES OF THE BROOKLYN SOUTH HOMICIDE SQUAD WERE IN THE Sixty-Seventh Precinct, on the second floor. I'd been there before, could have ducked into a staircase or elevator and gone up, but I decided to stop at the front desk and let them announce me.

"Delvecchio?" the salt-and-pepper haired sergeant asked.

"That's right."

"You a cop?"

"Used to be," I said. "Now I'm private."

"And who do you wanna see?"

"Detective Weinstock, Homicide."

"Hold on."

I didn't know if Weinstock would be catching this case, but he was the one I knew up there—actually, he was the one I knew would *talk* to me.

The sergeant got on the phone, said a few words, listened, then hung up.

"You know the way?" he asked.

"Unless you moved it."

"Naw," he said, "same place. Go ahead."

"Thanks, Sarge."

I took the stairs rather than wait for the elevator for one floor. When I entered the squad room I got some strange looks from the detectives but I walked through like I belonged there.

At the end of a row of desks sat Detective Weinstock. He was my age, seemed to give me more respect than most cops did. That included his asshole partner, Vito Matucci, who I knew from my seven years on the job.

Weinstock saw me coming, while Matucci had his back to me. He was echoing Matucci's sentiments and bitchin' about the Mets being twenty games out, even though they were in second place.

"Nick," Weinstock said, by way of greeting. "Sorry about your dad."

Matucci—who shared my father's first name—turned to look at me and said, grudgingly, "Yeah, sorry."

"Thanks, Vito," I said to Matucci. I looked at Weinstock. "You guys catch this?"

"No," Weinstock said, "we didn't. The whole case—your dad, Nicky Barracuda—is being handled by Sergeant Hicks and Detective Del Costa."

"I don't know them."

"They don't know you, either," Weinstock said. "I don't know if that's gonna work for you or against you, Nick."

"Why a sergeant?" I asked. "They don't usually catch cases."

"Because it's the Don," Matucci said.

"Is Hicks around? Or Del Costa?"

"Both," Weinstock said. "You want me to introduce you?"

"I'd appreciate it."

"I don't know if that'll help, either," Weinstock said. "He's not too fond of Jews." Weinstock pointed to himself.

"Or Italians," Matucci said.

"How's he feel about Mexicans?" I asked.

"He lumps us all in together," Weinstock said, standing up. "This guy's a pip, Nick. A throwback. I'd tell you to watch you p's and q's, but I know you too well for that. Come on."

Once again I walked the length of the squad room, but this time I was walking with Weinstock, so nobody paid me any mind.

As we approached a desk I saw the name plate with "Sgt. Andrew Hicks" written on it.

"Sarge, this is Nick Delvecchio," Weinstock said. "It was his dad who was killed yesterday in that Sheepshead Bay shooting."

Hicks looked up at Weinstock, then at me, with no expression. He had a bloated, drinker's face, making him look fifty when he was probably forty.

"Have a seat," he said to me.

I pulled over a chair.

"You can go back to your desk, Detective," Hicks said to Weinstock.

"I thought I'd sit in—" Weinstock said.

"I don't think so," Hicks said. "I'm sure you got your own case load."

Weinstock stood there a moment, then turned and walked back to his desk. I noticed all the other detectives in the room studiously avoided watching him.

"Mr. Delvecchio," Hicks said, "needless to say we're very sorry about your father—"

"Thank you."

"—personally, it woulda been no skin off my nose if Nick Barracuda had bought it instead."

"You'd have to investigate either way, though, right?" I asked.

"That's right," he said, "I would. And the outcome will probably be the same. I'll catch the bastards and they'll go down for murder."

"I'm glad to hear it," I said. "You mind me asking what you've got so far?"

Hicks sat back in his chair and took a long look at me.

"Look, I understand you used to be on the job, now you're private. I'm not obligated to fill you in on my investigation."

"No, you're not," I said. "I understand that."

"Good."

"I'm just here as a courtesy," I said. "First, to keep you from having to look for me and second, to arrange some sort of quid pro quo."

"Quid pro quo," Hicks said. "That means you're gonna be doin' some investigatin' of your own? On an active police investigation? That's a good way to risk losin' your license, you know."

"I'm aware of that," I said. "I didn't say I was going to investigate, but I might hear somethin' useful."

"Which you would naturally turn over to me, because you wanna see your father's killer caught. I don't see any quid pro quo in that, Mr. Delvecchio."

He had a point. I did want my father's killer caught, and if I heard anything at all I'd turn it over to him, even though I'd work the info myself. That didn't obligate him to me, at all. And he was also right that I would be putting my license at risk by working an active homicide case.

"Well then," I said, starting to stand, "I guess we don't have anything—"

"Hold on," Hicks said. "We do have some questions for you before you leave, if you don't mind."

I sat back in the chair.

"I don't mind."

"This is Detective Del Costa," he said, looking at somebody behind me. "We're workin' this case together."

I smelled her before I saw her. When I turned my head and saw the woman behind me I immediately stood up. She had thick black hair, dark eyebrows, red lipstick, tailored jacket and pants that did nothing to hide the fact that God had blessed her. I put her at about thirty-five.

"Angie," Hicks said, "this is Nick Delvecchio. It was his father who was killed in the Sheepshead Bay killin'."

"I'm sorry for your loss," she said, holding my eyes.

"Thanks."

"He was kind enough to come in so we wouldn't hafta go lookin' for him. Do a quick interview, will ya? Get what you can?"

"Sure, Sarge. Would you come this way to my desk, please?"

"Sure."

"Thanks for comin' in, Delvecchio," Hicks said.

I followed her to her desk, initially eyeing her from behind like any man would do, until I noticed that—once again—all the other men in the room were making a concerted effort not to watch her.

Twenty-Three

DETECTIVE ANGIE DEL COSTA WAS A LOOKER, AND NOBODY WAS LOOKING. It was odd, unless she and the sergeant had something going and everybody knew it. Most women in the department had to deal with that kind of unfair supposition, but I'm a firm believer that where there's smoke there's fire. In some cases, it had to be more than just supposition. Maybe this was one of them.

I risked a look over at Weinstock, who I thought was trying to send me some kind of message with a look. Unfortunately, I couldn't figure it out at that moment.

I ignored the fact that Detective Del Costa was a good-looking woman and treated her like just another detective.

She asked me a series of questions about my dad. What did he do for a living? Did he have any enemies? Did he associate with Nick Barracuda on a regular basis?

I said he was a longshoreman for years, he was retired, and yes.

"Did he do anything else?" she asked. "I mean, other than working the docks?"

"For a long time he was a union rep."

"Ah." She furiously made a note.

"Detective, you are acting on the assumption that Nicky Barracuda was the target, aren't you?"

She looked at me and smiled. One of her front teeth had a smear of red lipstick on it.

"We're looking at every option, Mr. Delvecchio."

"You're not from Brooklyn," I said.

"No," she said, "I'm not originally from New York. I'm from Connecticut."

"There's no chance my dad was the target, here," I told her.

"As I said, sir, we're looking at every option."

She asked if I had seen my father yesterday, before he went to Sheepshead Bay for lunch? Had I spoken to him? Had I spoken to Mr. Barracondi lately?

I said no, no, and no.

I noticed during the interview that Weinstock got up and left the squad room. By the time Del Costa was done with me he hadn't come back.

"Okay, Mr. Delvecchio," she said, handing me an embossed business card, "if you hear anything useful we'd appreciate a call."

"Sure," I said, taking the card.

I ceased to exist for her, then, so I stood up and left.

I found Weinstock waiting for me outside the building.

"Just a word to the wise," he said. "Del Costa is Hicks's private stock."

"What's that mean, exactly?"

"Protégé, punchboard, whatever you want it to mean."

"You know this for a fact?"

"Yep," he said. "Word is she got tired of fighting her way to the top."

"So she decided to sleep her way?" I asked. "With a sergeant?"

"Hicks knows where a lot of bodies are buried," Weinstock said. "And he likes being a sergeant."

"So he's a user."

"Don't kid yourself," Weinstock said. "So is she."

"You sayin' they deserve each other."

"I'm saying watch your step. I saw you watching her step."

"I'm not lookin' to get laid, Weinstock," I said. "I'm lookin' for my dad's killer."

"Well, just watch yourself around those two."

"What's your lieutenant got to say about all this?"

He laughed and said, "Wake me when it's time for my pension," and went back inside.

Twenty-Four

SHEEPSHEAD BAY WAS NEXT. FISHING BOATS, RESTAURANTS, DINERS, A FEW shops here and there.

What confused me was why were Nicky Barracuda and my father eating at Rizzo's—at a sidewalk table while the Don owned a restaurant called On The Barge, and usually ate his meals at his own place.

Both the Barge and Rizzo's were on the Bay's main drag, Emmons Avenue, but on opposite sides of the street, and several blocks apart.

I went to Rizzo's, which was serving lunch. The shooting must have made a mess of the windows, but they had already been replaced. Business must go on. I went inside and was approached by a maître d'.

"One, sir?"

"I'm not here to eat," I said. "I have some questions about the shooting yesterday." I figured let him think I was either a cop or a hood. Either one worked for me. "Were you working yesterday?"

"Oh, yes, sir."

"So you were here during the shooting?"

"Such a terrible tragedy," he said. "Those poor men."

"What's your name?"

"Salvatore."

"Did you know the two men?"

"No, sir."

Salvatore was sweating. His bald head was gleaming with it, and one drop ran down from his temple to his cheek. It was hot for spring, but not that hot.

"Come on, Sal," I said. "You know who one of them was. I know you do."

"Sir . . ." he said, nervously, "I'm not lookin' for any trouble."

"Are you the owner?"

"No, sir."

"Is he here?"

"He's in his office."

"Was he here yesterday, when the shooting took place?" I asked.

"No, sir."

"Okay, stop calling me 'sir,'" I said.

"Yes, s—"

"I'm not a cop," I said.

"I didn't think you were."

Oh, I got it.

"I'm not a wise guy, either," I said. "Look, let's go inside so you can relax. I only have a few questions."

"I don't understand," he said, "if you're not a cop and you're not . . ."

"One of the men who was shot was my father," I said. "He died."

"Oh . . ."

"Inside, Sal."

We went inside where it was cooler. It was not a heavy lunch crowd. I directed him to the bar and called the bartender over.

"Get Sal some cold water, please."

"Something for you, sir?" the bartender asked.

"No—yeah, bring me a Peroni."

"Yes, sir."

"Now Sal," I said, "you know very well who one of the men was."

"Yes, s—yes," he said. "Mr. Barracondi. We were very surprised to see him here."

"Why's that?"

"Because he always eats at his own restaurant."

"Good," I said, "you know that much. Now, tell me what you saw."

The bartender came over with his water, and my bottle of beer. Sal drank half the water down. I sipped the beer.

"I didn't see anything. I was inside when the windows shattered. I didn't even know there was shooting until later."

"Did you go outside at all?"

He looked embarrassed.

"I ducked behind the bar and stayed there until the police came."

Great.

"What about their waiter?"

"That was Frankie."

"And where's Frankie right now?"

"H-he didn't come in today."

"Did he call in sick?"

"No, he just didn't show up."

"Did he talk to the police yesterday?"

"Yeah," Sal said. "We all did."

"Then I'm gonna need Frankie's address."

"Excuse me, but if you're not the police . . ."

"I'm a private investigator," I said. "The man killed was my father. I need that address. I can pay you for it, or I can threaten you."

"Just a minute."

He left me at the bar for ten minutes, but instead of reappearing, another man came over to me.

"Mr. Delvecchio?"

"Yes?"

"My name is Rizzo, Joseph Rizzo. Would you be kind enough to come unto my office?"

"Can you help me?" I asked. "I assume Sal told you what I'm looking for."

"Yes, of course," Rizzo said. He was slick, but with hair gel, not sweat. "Please?"

"Lead the way."

I followed his wide back, tailored suit and bald spot, taking my beer with me. He led me into the back to an office, closing the door after we entered.

"Have a seat, Mr. Delvecchio," he said. He sat behind his desk. He picked up an index card from his desk top. In fact, other than a lamp it was the only thing on his desk. There was a computer on another table next to him.

"I have here the address you're looking for," he said. "Our waiter, Frankie?"

"Frankie who?"

"Frankie . . ." he frowned at the card. " . . . DiGuardi."

"And how much is it gonna cost me?"

"Not a thing. Well, not money."

"What, then?"

He sat forward.

"All I want you to do," he said, "is tell Nicky Barracuda that Joey Rizzo was . . . helpful to you in a time of need."

"That's it?"

"That's it." He sat back.

"I can do that."

He smiled, and handed me the card.

"And the beer's on the house," he said, as I went out the door.

Twenty-Five

FRANKIE THE WAITER LIVED IN THE BASEMENT OF A TWO-FAMILY HOUSE in Marine Park, which was only about a fifteen-minute ride to work for him.

I parked a few doors down from Frankie's address and walked back. I went through a freshly painted wrought-iron gate and down four concrete steps to the doorway that was beneath the front steps of the house. This time of day the block was quiet, no kids at play because they were still in school. I passed one young mother pushing a baby carriage, but she didn't pay any attention to me. She only had eyes for her little angel, who was screaming his or her lungs out.

I rang the doorbell and waited. There was one window that I could see, but it had an air-conditioner in it, so I couldn't see into the basement apartment.

I rang the doorbell a second time, then opened the screen door and knocked on a wooden door that had no peephole in it.

With a bad feeling I tried the doorknob. It turned. The door was unlocked. Since the police had already spoken with Frankie at the scene the day before, there would have been no reason for them to come and talk to him today.

"Crap," I said. Anybody who watched TV or movies would know I was gonna find a body inside. I knew it. I also knew I should probably call the police, but I decided to make sure first.

"Crapcrapcrap," I muttered, and opened the door.

When I stepped inside I was immediately chilled. The air-conditioner in the window must have been set on high, because it was freezing.

"Hello?" I called. "Frankie?"

No answer.

"Come on, man," I pleaded, "don't be dead."

Nothing.

There was a second door, but it was already wide open. I stepped through into the basement apartment. It looked like it had been partitioned off into three rooms, shotgun style. I was in the living room with a sofa and some bookshelves, but not much else. No sign of Frankie there. There were some posters on the wall, one of lady bodybuilding champion Cory Everson. Another was a poster of New York Yankee great Don Mattingly, who was probably playing his last season due to back problems.

I could see through to the small kitchen.

It was the room in between I was concerned with. I took four steps across the room, spotted the single bed against the wall and the body on it, tangled in the sheets.

He hadn't been dead long or I would have smelled him, or the blood, when I came in. He was lying face down on the bed, a single bullet hole in the back of his head. Maybe somebody who dealt with gunshot deaths more than I had would have smelled the residue in the air from the gunpowder. Or felt the body and figured out how long he'd been dead. Standing this close to him I could smell the blood, but the rest was beyond me.

Obviously, Frankie knew something that had gotten him killed. He either saw something yesterday, or he'd been involved from the start. Maybe he'd made a phone call when Pop and the Barracuda first sat down.

I did a quick search of the apartment, knowing I wouldn't find anything. The shooter must have removed anything incriminating. He was good at his job.

Now I had to get myself out of there without being seen.

There was a bathroom, and next to it another door. I opened it and found myself in a boiler room that led to a back door. I used my shirt tail and wiped off anything I might have touched, then pulled the apartment door closed behind me.

I went out the building's back door, found myself in a backyard, climbed a couple of fences and came out on a street around the corner. I got back to my car and drove away. I prayed there were no busybodies peering out their windows, taking down license numbers. Hoped I hadn't contaminated the crime scene.

Either thing would leave me a lot of 'splainin' to do.

Twenty-Six

I HAD A DECISION TO MAKE: PLACE AN ANONYMOUS CALL TO THE COPS, or let somebody else find the body.

By the time I got to the hospital I'd decided not to make a call. I parked, went inside and took the elevator to the Don's floor. When I came out I could see down the hall that there was still a cop on the door. Once again I had to identify myself to be let in. The guard studied me for a long minute and I wondered if I'd gotten blood on my nose or something. My heart started to pound, and then he let me pass.

Benny turned and looked. I could see the tension in his face and body, but he relaxed when he saw me.

"You react that way every time somebody comes in?" I asked.

"Yeah," he said. "The Don's life is in my hands."

"Must scare the hell out of the nurses."

He shrugged his massive shoulders.

"How is he?" I said.

"In and out."

"Say anything?"

"No."

"The detectives been by?"

"Yeah, some sergeant named Hicks and a hot-lookin' lady detective." He frowned for a moment, then said, "I think he's doin' her."

"So the Don hasn't made a statement to anybody yet?"

"No. Where you been?"

"Sheepshead Bay."

"Find out anythin'?"

I turned and looked at the door, lowered my voice, and told him about Frankie the waiter.

"You call the cops?"

"No," I said. "I'm gonna let somebody else find the body."

"That's cool. Better to stay out of it. You talk to Joey Rizzo?" he asked.

"Yeah. He gave me the address."

"What'd he want for it?"

"Nothin', except for me to put a good word in for him with the Don."

"That figures."

"Rizzo connected?"

"No. He just runs a restaurant. He ain't a wise guy, no matter how much he wants ta be."

"Tell me somethin', Benny," I said. "Why were the Don and Pop eatin' at Rizzo's and not on the Barge?"

"I don't know," Benny said with a shrug. "The Don just told me he was goin' to Rizzo's to meet your dad."

"To meet?" I asked. "So they didn't go there together?"

"No. Me and the Don walked. Your dad was already there."

"How did he get there?"

"I don't know. I figured he drove."

"No, he doesn't—didn't—have a license, anymore. He had cataracts."

"Can't they fix that, these days?"

"He wouldn't go for the operation," I said. "Stubborn. Said he didn't trust doctors to go pokin' around in his eyes."

"I can understand that," Benny said, looking around the room. "I don't like doctors or hospitals, myself."

"Why did you and the Don walk? Doesn't he still have a driver?"

"Yeah, but he said it was a nice day and he wanted to walk."

"So anybody could've taken a shot at him during the walk," I said.

"The shooters might have been watchin' the restaurant," Benny suggested.

"How would they know he was gonna be there? Did he make a

reservation?" We were speaking in the plural, even though we didn't know if there had been more than one shooter.

"No, no reservation."

"I figure the dead waiter must've fingered him," I said.

"But why?"

"Why else? Money."

"That would mean the word went out on the hit," Benny said. "Money was offered for somebody to finger the Don." Benny was getting mad.

"Can you find out about that?"

"I can try," he said. "Nobody's gonna tell me they was willin' to finger the Don. They know I'd kill 'em. But somebody might talk and give somebody else up. Unless they're too scared to."

"You're right," I said. "We need somebody else to do the asking."

"Lemme give it some thought."

I nodded.

"You sure nobody saw you at the waiter's place?" he asked.

"As sure as I can be," I said. "I didn't see anybody, so I'm hopin' the vice is versa."

"Huh?"

"I hope nobody saw me."

"Oh."

"Have you eaten today?"

"No," Benny said. "I ain't left this room."

"I'll go get you somethin'," I said.

He grabbed my arm as I turned.

"Nicky, not from the cafeteria," he said, almost pleadingly.

"Okay. Burger King?" I asked. "I saw one down the street."

"That's good. A whopper. With fries, and a large coke. Oh, and a shake."

"What flavor?"

He looked at me like I was crazy and said, "Chocolate."

"And do you want the burger your way or theirs?" I asked.

Twenty-Seven

I CAME BACK WITH A WHOPPER AND FRIES FOR BENNY, AND A CHICKEN sandwich and fries for me. I had asked the cop on the door if he wanted anything, so I brought him a Whopper meal, too.

Benny and I sat on either side of the Don's bed and ate. A nurse came in at one point, a young one. She steered away from Benny, giving him a frightened look, and came around to my side of the bed to check on the Don's readings.

"Fry?" I asked, offering the box.

She giggled, took two and ate them.

"Don't tell anyone," she said.

"I won't."

"Neither will I," Benny said.

She looked at him, gave him a tentative smile, said, "Thanks," and left.

"She won't be so scared of you now," I said.

Around a mouthful of fries he asked, "She's scared of me?"

"Most people are, Benny."

Before he could say anything the Don moaned, moved his head, then reached for the oxygen mask.

"Hey, don't—" Benny said, but the old man was determined.

"W-when . . ." he managed.

"Yesterday," I told him.

He looked at me, then back at Benny, then almost smiled. "My boys." Then Benny put the mask back over the Don's nose and mouth.

"That's all he does," Benny told me. "In and out."

"How many bullets hit him?"

"Three."

"They said four hit my dad," I said. "It was either a car full of guys with guns . . ."

". . . or one guy with a machine gun."

"The cops know and aren't telling us," I said.

"That Hicks is an asshole."

"Give you a hard time?"

"He tried."

"What about the woman? Del Costa?"

"Didn't say much," he said. "I think she only talks when he says somethin' to her, or gives her the okay. She could be a hot piece of ass if she dressed different. What's she doin' with him?"

"Makin' a career move, I've been told."

"Some career."

I put my Burger King garbage in the bag and dropped it in the trash. Benny did the same.

"I better get movin'," I said.

"Where ya goin' next?"

"That depends on you," I said. "Give me a name. Somebody who's got their ear to the ground and isn't afraid to talk about what he hears."

He thought a minute, and then said, "There's a guy named Winky Manzo."

"Winky?"

"Yeah, don't worry about that. If there's word on the street, this guy'll know it."

"Where do I find him?"

"You'll have to let him find you."

"And how do I do that?"

"I got a couple of places you can go and say you're lookin' for him," he said. "After that you'll just hafta wait."

"How long, Benny?" I asked. "I don't want this trail goin' cold."

"Don't worry," he said. "He'll get back to ya. Meantime, ain't there somethin' else you can do?"

Actually, there was.

Twenty-Eight

I WENT BACK TO MY OFFICE. SAM MUST HAVE HEARD MY DOOR CLOSE because just moments later she entered. When I'm at my desk I don't keep the office door locked.

"You okay?" she asked, sticking her head in.

"I'm fine," I said, then added, "for now."

She entered, closed the door behind her.

"How's your, uh, uncle?"

"The same," I said. "Hasn't fully woke up, yet, so the cops haven't gotten a statement from him. Neither have I."

"Have you found out anything?"

I decided not to let her in on the dead waiter.

"Not much. I'm waitin' for some calls."

"What are you going to do while you wait?" she asked.

"Actually, I'm also gonna make some calls. I've got to find out how my dad got to the restaurant."

"His cataracts wouldn't let him drive," she said.

"You've got a good memory. That's right, so I've got to find a car service that took him. That means callin' all the ones who serve that area."

"You need my phone?"

"No, I have two lines here."

"How about something to eat?"

"I just had some Burger King with Benny."

She made a face.

"If you're still here at dinner time I'll make something."

"That'd be great."

"Nick, can you give me a phone number for your brother and your sister. I'd like to give them my condolences."

"Sure." I wrote down a bunch of numbers. "Try my dad's number first. They might still be there."

"Thanks. I'll see you later."

"Thanks, Sam."

As she left I looked at my message machine. It was blinking convulsively. I pressed play.

First one was from Tony Mitts: "Nick, I ain't heard from you. What's goin' on?"

Second from Mary Ann's mother: "Nick, I just heard about your father. I'm so sorry. Listen, you don't have to continue looking into Mary Ann's death. Y-you have enough to worry about. I'll understand."

Third was my sister, Maria: "Nick? We're still at Pop's. Call us and let us know you're okay."

Tony again: "Aw, jeez, Nick, I just heard. I'm really sorry . . . but d'ya think you can still work on Mary Ann's death? I know, I sound like an asshole, but . . . aw, jeez—" Click.

Then Benny: "I put the word out to Winky, Nick. Give him a chance to call ya, then go and check out those places I todja about. The Don's okay, he's breathin' good."

Finally, one from an anonymous voice: "Delvecchio, I might have somethin' for ya about Nicky Barracuda's shootin'. I'll call ya again, but we gotta meet if you want my info. And it won't be free."

If that had been Benny's guy, Winky, he would've said so. That meant somebody out there thought he had something to sell. I'd have to wait and see.

I called Maria, caught her and Father Vinnie at my dad's. I told her I was okay and that I was working on the shooting.

"Don't do anything stupid, Nicky. You hear me?" she said.

"I hear you, Maria," I said. "Nothin' stupid. I promise."

I hung up, pulled out a Yellow Pages and started looking up car services.

A couple of hours later I closed the phone book. I'd run out of companies to call. None had made a pickup at Pop's address. It was too far for him to walk to Sheepshead Bay. That left two possibilities.

He took the bus.

Or somebody picked him up and drove him there.

"Delvecchio?"

"That's me."

I was about to check with Sam on her promise to cook when the phone rang. It was the same anonymous voice.

"You investigatin' the shootin' of Nicky Barracuda?" he asked.

"How would you know that?" I asked.

"I asked around. I got some info for ya."

"Why don't you give it to the cops?"

"I don't talk to no scumbag cops."

"And they wouldn't pay you."

"You got that right."

"Well, I've got to tell you I don't have much money. I'm just a hard workin' P.I."

"Yeah, but you can get it."

"What makes you think that?"

"Because you and the Don, you gotta—whatayacallit—a bond."

"Who've you been talkin' to?" I asked.

"Look, if ya don't want the info it's no skin offa my nose. I'm just tryin' to make a few bucks, here. And help you out at the same time."

"Okay, okay," I said, "when can we meet?"

"Can you get the money by tonight?"

"How much are we talkin' about?"

"Five G's oughtta do it."

I was suspicious. Five thousand dollars did not seem like enough for somebody who was trying to squeeze me.

"I'll get it," I said. "Where do we meet?"

"I'll call ya tonight around nine," he said. "If you got the money, I'll tell ya where ta meet me."

That gave me a few hours to come up with the five grand.

"Okay," I said. "I'll wait for your call."

He hung up without saying another word.

I went next door to see what Sam had cooking.

Twenty-Nine

SAM MADE A POT ROAST, WHICH WAS FINE WITH ME. I'D HAD HER COOKING before, and it was great. This was no different.

Over dinner I told her about the call.

"You're going to meet him tonight?"

"Yeah."

"Alone?"

"Not necessarily."

"And where are you going to get five thousand dollars?"

"That's already been taken care of," I said. "It's being delivered here in a couple of hours."

"You made a call and got five thousand dollars in two hours?"

I nodded and said, "I've got connections."

Yeah, connections named Benny. The five grand was the Don's money, and Benny was sending it over with the Don's driver.

Now the question was, who was gonna watch my back?

I was in my office, waiting for the money to be delivered — hopefully, before the phone call. When the phone rang it was too soon.

"Nicky? Hey, it's Tony."

Great.

"Hello, Tony."

"How you doin', buddy?"

"I'm doin' okay."

"I was really sorry to hear about your dad. I feel really bad about the messages I left."

"That's okay, Tony. You didn't know."

"Yeah, thanks. Uh, so what's goin' on? The cops lookin' into your dad's death?"

"Yeah, they are," I said, "but so am I."

"Oh." He sounded disappointed.

"Tony . . . look . . ."

"Nicky, man . . . I was countin' on you . . . so was Mary Ann's mom."

"Yeah," I said, "that was kinda before my dad got killed, Tony."

"Look," he said, "I feel like a shit, okay?"

"Mary Ann's mom called me, Tony. She told me to forget it. She'd understand."

"Yeah, she would," he said, "she's like that. She's definitely a better person than me."

Jesus.

"Look, Tony," I said, "I may have some time tomorrow to do . . . something. I want to talk to Mary Ann's mom again, about the rape."

"Rape?" he asked. "What rape?"

I couldn't believe I did that. I forgot that Tony didn't know about the rape.

"Nick? Whataya talkin' about?"

"I heard that Mary Anna was raped, Tony."

"I never—she never said—who told you that?"

"I'm not gonna tell you that right now."

"Then who did it?"

"I'm not tellin' you that, either, Tony," I said. "You'll go off half-cocked."

"I won't go off half-cocked," he said. "I'll just kill the bastard! My Mary Ann was raped? Are you shittin' me, Nick?"

There was a knock on my door at that moment.

"Tony I gotta go. Somebody's at the door."

"Nick! Don't you hang up—"

I hung up.

Then opened the door.

The Don's driver was standing there with a brown envelope.

"Five G's," he said, handing it to me.

"Okay, thanks."

He didn't move.

"Somethin' else?"

"Benny said I was to drive you wherever you wanna go," he said.

He was dressed all in black, with dark glasses and a black chauffer's cap. If I hadn't recognized him I might've acted differently.

"What's your name?"

"Carlo."

"Okay, Carlo. I'm not quite ready to go yet. You wanna come in and wait?"

"If it's okay, I'll wait in the car."

"It's fine with me," I said. I looked at my watch. It was almost eight. "I'll see you in a while."

He nodded and walked down the hall. I took the money back to my desk. The phone rang and I had a feeling it was Tony, so I let the machine pick up.

"Nicky, you prick," Tony said. "You can't tell me my Mary Ann was raped and then hang—"

I disconnected. I didn't have time to deal with Tony's outrage.

The phone rang again.

Thirty

I GOT INTO THE BACK OF THE DON'S LIMO AND SAID, "CANARSIE."

"Canarsie?"

I nodded.

"Where?"

"East a hundred and eighth street and Avenue N," I said.

"What's there?" he asked.

"We'll find out when we get there."

He shrugged and said, "Okay."

He started the car and off we went to South Brooklyn.

"You got a gun?" I asked from the back seat as we drove.

"I'm just a driver."

"Yeah, but you drive the Don," I said. "You do that unarmed?"

"Well . . . Benny's always with us."

And Benny was always armed.

Carlo pulled the car to a stop at our destination. It was a pool club for the locals to bring their kids, spend their summer days sunning, swimming and—for all anyone knew—swapping.

Carlo turned in his seat and looked at me.

"This ain't it," he said.

"I know," I said. "How do *you* know?"

He pointed his gun at me.

"Cut the crap," he said. "How'd you know it was me? I disguised my voice."

"Not very well. Rich Little you ain't."

I figured after he handed me the money and went down to his car he'd gone to a pay phone and called me. I know the sounds of my own neighborhood, and they had come to me in the background. Also, it made sense. Who else would know something but somebody close to the Don?

But I wasn't dead sure, so I gave Carlo a different location than the one he'd given me on the phone.

And he'd lied about his gun.

"Why not just take the five grand when Benny gave it to you?" I asked.

"Then he'd know I took it," Carlo said. "This way . . ."

"How were you gonna do it?"

"Let you out, wait until you were out of sight, then get out of the car and meet you."

"Wearing a mask?"

He held up a ski mask in his other hand, then dropped it.

"Okay, then," I said, "what've you got, Carlo?"

"The money first."

I took the envelope out of my windbreaker jacket and handed it over the seat. He riffled the contents with his thumb.

"It's all there," I said.

"Didn't slip one or two bills out for yourself?"

"No."

He studied me, then said, "Yeah, you wouldn't." Without the dark glasses I could see he was in his early thirties, with startling blue eyes. Trying to build himself a nest egg, maybe.

"Okay, Carlo, so talk to me."

"The Barge."

"What about it?"

"I can let you on it," he said. "Let you into the Don's office."

"Why would I want to go there?"

"Check it out," he said. "The Don got a call that day. I was in the room. He got a call, then told me to step out. After that he told me he didn't need me to drive him."

"And you think that was because of the call?"

"Yeah."

"And you're thinkin' maybe he wrote somethin' down?" I asked.

"He don't remember things so good no more," Carlo said. "He makes notes."

I thought about it. It made sense. If he went to the restaurant to meet somebody, though, why was my dad there, too?

"Okay," I said. "Take me."

"What, now?"

"Why not?"

"Well . . . it's late."

"You got a date?"

"No."

"Somethin' else to do?"

"Well, no but—"

"So let's go, Carlo," I said, sitting back. "Drive."

"What about Benny?" he asked. "You won't tell him about this, will you?"

"No," I said, "no reason to tell him."

"Okay, then."

He lowered his gun, turned and started the car. Sheepshead Bay was only a couple of exits away on the Belt Parkway.

I released my gun and took my hand out of my jacket pocket.

Thirty-One

CARLO UNLOCKED THE DOOR OF THE BARGE AND WE ENTERED.

"Does Benny know you have a key?"

"No," he said. "The Don gave it to me the last time he forgot his. He's been gettin' forgetful."

We walked through the restaurant part, where the chairs were stacked on top of the tables. I knew the way to the Don's office. Carlo followed me. It occurred to me that I was letting a guy with a gun get behind me, but I didn't think he was in on the Don's shooting . . . and I had my own piece.

When we got to the office we entered and turned on the light. The Don's desk was immaculate. I wasn't going to find any notes on top of it, that was for sure.

I went around and sat down. Benny would have been appalled.

Carlo sat across from me and watched while I went through the desk drawers. The middle one was filled with slips of paper, the Don's scrawl all over them.

"I see what you mean by notes," I said. I scooped them out and laid them on the desk. Yellow and blue post it notes, torn scraps of paper, even pages torn from magazines and newspapers. All with scribbling on them.

"Gonna read them here?" Carlo asked.

"Too many."

I went through the other drawers. Apparently the Don kept all his notes in one. I found an empty 8x11 brown envelope and swept all the scraps into it.

I did a quick scan of his desk top but there was nothing there.

"What about his files?" Carlo said.

I looked over at the single file cabinet in the room. I stood up and tried the drawer, found it locked.

"You got a key for this, too?" I asked.

"Naw," he said. "Pick it."

It would have taken me a while without lock picks.

"Benny should have a key," I said. "If I got in here now I wouldn't know what I was lookin' for. I can get into it later if I have to."

Carlo shrugged. He didn't care. He had his five grand.

"Let's blow," I said. "Drive me back home?"

"Sure, why not?"

Moments later, as we left the Barge and walked back onto the dock, I found out why not.

There was a shot, and Carlo went down.

Thirty-Two

CARLO MADE A SOUND AS HE WENT DOWN, BUT THE WAY HE HIT THE ground I knew he was dead. There was a finality about it.

I hit the concrete of the dock and rolled, trying to get my gun out of my jacket. The hammer snagged and I ended up ripping the pocket.

There wasn't much cover for me. I either had to go into the water, try to get back on the Barge, or use Carlo's body. But for the moment I was a clear target and nobody was shooting at me. Was Carlo the intended target? If so the shooter was very good at his job. Took Carlo out with a single shot, and then got out quick.

I took a chance, stood up and moved back toward the Barge. There was no shot, so I stopped at the base of the gangway, where Carlo was lying. I bent down to take a look at him. He'd been shot in the heart, the bullet going right through the envelope of money.

Another dead body for me to deal with. I'd left the waiter for someone else to find, but this was different. We were out in the open, the shot had been loud. Even though I couldn't see anyone it didn't mean there wasn't someone out in the dark looking at me. Plus, to get away from there I'd have to lift Carlo's keys and use the limo.

I decided to get to a phone and call the cops. Not 911, though. I was going to call Sergeant Hicks directly. Or Detective Del Costa.

I walked up the dock to the street to find a pay phone, feeling like I had a bullseye painted on me.

•

IT TURNED out to be Del Costa. Although she'd been dragged out of bed she looked perfect, hair and make-up expertly applied, wearing another tailored suit. She arrived with the precinct sector car for that area. They got out and left their turret lights flashing.

"Where's your boss?" I asked.

"I called him," she said. "Whataya got?"

"Shooting," I said. "Over here."

As we walked up the dock, the two uniforms in tow, she asked, "What are you doing here this late?"

"Just checking the place out," I said. "The Don's in the hospital, and so's his man. I was just checking to make sure the place was secure."

"You get inside?"

"We were inside, and when we came out there was a shot."

"Who's we?"

"The Don's driver, Carlo. Came to pick me up and take me over."

"A little bodyguarding, too?"

"If he was he didn't do a very good job, did he?"

"He's the one who's dead, right?"

She had a point.

When we reached the body she called for the uniforms to shine their maglights on the body. She checked him, heard the rustling inside his coat and pulled out the envelope.

"Looks like a wad of cash," she said to me. "You know anything about it?"

"He didn't take it from inside," I said. "We were together the whole time."

She looked me up and down. I had stashed my envelope full of scribbled notes in the back seat of the limo.

I raised my hands.

"Wanna check?"

"No," she said, handing the bloody envelope to one of the cops. "Tell me again what happened?"

I did, exactly the way it had happened. There was nothing for me to hide.

"One shot?" she asked. "He got it in the heart. That was good shooting."

"I know."

"You armed, Delvecchio?"

I took my gun out, using two fingers so the cops didn't get nervous, and handed it to her. She sniffed it, then handed it back.

"What about him?" she asked.

"I didn't ask, but it looked like he had a piece under his arm."

She squatted again, reached in and pulled his gun out. It was a .38, much like mine. She stood, smelled it, then handed it to one of the cops, who used his pen through the trigger guard to take it from her.

We all noticed headlights as another car joined the flashing lights at the front of the dock.

"Sergeant's here," one of the cops said.

"Wait here," she said. "All of you."

She walked to meet Hicks halfway. The two cops were watching her ass, so I joined in. She spoke with her partner, then they walked over to us together.

"Delvecchio," he said, "we're gonna need you to come in and make a statement."

"No problem."

He looked down at the body with his hands in his jacket pockets. He was wearing a windbreaker similar to mine. Unlike his partner, he looked like he'd rolled out of bed and dressed in a hurry.

"One shot, huh?" he asked. He turned to look at me. "And you didn't see anythin'?"

"Not even a muzzle flash."

"Why didn't you call it in to nine-one-one?" he asked.

"You're workin' the Don's shooting," I said. "I figured you'd want in on this."

"Okay, come on," he said. "You'll ride in with us. Where's your car?"

"He drove the Don's limo," I said, indicating Carlo's body. "It's parked."

"Okay, we'll leave it. Anythin' in there you need?"

"Nope," I lied, "I've got everything I need on me."

Hicks looked at his partner.

"Take him in," he said. "I'll wait for the M.E. and see you there."

She nodded and said to me, "This way."

Thirty-Three

TWO HOURS LATER I WAS SITTING AT DEL COSTA'S DESK, SIGNING MY statement. Hicks had still not returned from Sheepshead Bay. The evidence—Carlo's gun, and the bloody envelope of money—would have been taken to the Sixty-Second Precinct, so maybe he was trying to get it from them. Or the M.E. may have taken a long time to respond. In addition, Hicks would have had to wait for a boss to arrive, most likely a Captain.

I signed the statement and pushed it across the desk to Del Costa.

"Okay, thanks." She looked it over briefly, then said, "You can go."

"That's it?"

"That's it."

"I've got a question," I said.

She stared at me and said, "What?" I had a feeling she thought she knew what I was going to ask.

She was wrong.

"It's about my father," I said. "Have you found out how he got to that restaurant?"

"No," she said. "He didn't drive, and we haven't found a car service that took him. We're checking cabs, now, but we're not hopeful. He may have gotten a ride from someone."

"That's what I was thinkin'," I said.

"Any idea who?"

"Normally, he'd ask me or my brother or my sister," I said. "But none of us took him."

"What's that like?" she asked.

"What?"

"Your brother," she said. "What's it like having a priest in the family?"

"Are you Catholic?"

"Yes, I am."

"Well, it ain't all it's cracked up to be," I said. "I don't go to Mass, so I always have to defend myself to him."

"What do you have against Mass?" she asked. "Or is it God?"

"I don't have a problem with God," I said. "I'm not real crazy about the Church."

"Aren't they the same thing?"

"Not to me."

"Hmm," she said.

"You go to Mass regularly?"

"No."

"Confession?"

She colored and said, "No."

"Me, neither. It's been years."

"How'd your dad feel about that?"

"We didn't discuss it," I said. "Not for a long, long time."

I stood up.

"You want a ride home?"

I didn't. I wanted to go back to Sheepshead Bay and get that envelope out of the limo, but it was probably too soon for that.

"Sure."

"I'll take you myself," she said.

"Hey, you're busy —"

"Don't worry about it," she said. "I'll probably go right home after that."

"You won't have to come back here?"

"Hicks will be handling things," she said.

We walked down the stairs to the main floor, and out the door.

"Sorry I had to wake you," I said.

"That's the job," she said. "You know, you did it for a while."

"A while."

We walked to her car. It was dark and quiet, I could hear her heels on the ground. She was tall, and her stride was equal to mine.

"My parents would've loved it if my brother became a priest," she said, out of the blue as we approached her car.

"Oh? What did he become, instead?"

"Dead," she said.

She drove in silence for a while, then said, "He was murdered when I was a teenager."

"Cops find out who did it?"

"No," she said. "I guess maybe that's why I became a cop."

"How'd it happen?"

"He was playing basketball in a schoolyard and a couple of guys came up and shot him."

"Witnesses?"

"The other players, but they claimed they didn't know the shooters."

My first thought was drugs, but I kept my opinion to myself.

"That's too bad," I said. "I know what it's like to lose a brother."

"You, too?"

"My oldest was killed in Viet Nam."

"That must have been tough."

"It was," I said, nodding. "My mother died a few years later, but it's my brother that my father has a small shrine to."

"That could be . . . creepy."

"Tell me about it."

"So Father Vincent is older than you?"

I nodded. "And Maria is the youngest."

"I have a younger sister, but Robert was my only brother."

We drove a while longer in silence. I was sure she didn't have time to put on perfume, but the car smelled like her, anyway.

"When did you get your shield?"

"A couple of years ago," she said. "It took me eight years."

"That's an accomplishment."

"Is it?" she asked, sounding almost bitter. "That depends on how you got it, doesn't it?"

"I just assumed you'd earned it."

She gave me a quick look before turning her attention back to the road.

"That's not the general opinion."

"What's it matter what anybody thinks as long as you know you earned it?"

She was quiet again until we pulled up in front of my place.

"I want to tell you something," she said.

"What?"

"I'm not sleeping with Hicks."

"It's no skin off my nose if you are."

"I know," she said. "That's why I wanted to tell you."

"But he is your rabbi, right?" When you had somebody in the department who was superior to you, and they helped your career, they were your "rabbi."

"We have an agreement," she said. "We let people think what they're going to think, and he helps me."

"Hey," I said, "you gotta do what you gotta do."

My reply didn't seem to be what she wanted. She turned and stared out the windshield.

"Look, I'm sorry," I said. "But if you want to know the truth, I really never thought you were sleepin' with him."

"What?" She looked at me and blinked.

"You're way too classy for him," I said. "Anybody who can't see that is an idiot."

"I—well—thank you."

"Thanks for the ride."

I started to get out, then paused and looked at her.

"What?" she said.

"Can I ask somethin' else about the case?"

"Sure, why not?" she asked. "We're bonding here, right?"

"Yeah, uh, right," I said. "Did you determine what kind of a gun was used on my dad?"

She hesitated, then said, "From the shells we recovered we figure they were shot with an Uzi."

"An Uzi?"

"Yeah, why?"

"Nothin'," I said. "Thanks."

"Look—" she said, then stopped.

"What?"

"Never mind. Keep in touch . . . about the case, I mean."

"I'm not looking into it, you know," I said.

"Yeah," she said, "sure. Just let us know if you hear anything."

"Will do."

Thirty-Four

THE MESSAGE LIGHT WAS GOING LIKE CRAZY.

I had a feeling most of the calls were going to be from an incensed Tony Mitts. And I figured he had a right to be mad. I was going to have to do something, since I had opened my big mouth. But I still needed to get back to Sheepshead Bay to get those notes from the limo. And I needed to let Benny know what had happened at the Barge. But I also needed to get a few hours' sleep or I'd be no good to anybody.

I fell into bed without even getting undressed. . . .

I woke as daylight came through my window. I could have used a few more hours, but I got up and showered and made myself a quick breakfast of coffee and toast. I got dressed, switched to my other windbreaker, once again stuck my .38 in the pocket. There was just too much lead flying around for me to go unarmed.

I left my apartment as quietly as possible. I didn't want Sam to hear me because I didn't want to take the time to explain everything to her. I could do that later.

I got my car, a five-year-old Toyota I'd picked up cheap, out of the parking lot where I kept it and aimed it at Sheepshead Bay. I still had Carlo's keys in my pocket, which was the only thing I'd lifted from his body before the cops arrived.

I drove down Emmons Avenue once without stopping, just to make sure there were no cops around. Second time I pulled in behind the limo, got out and quickly retrieved the envelope from the back seat. I locked the car, got back in mine and drove to Victory Memorial to see Benny and let him know what had happened.

"Carlo's dead?" he asked.

"Yeah," I said, "and that's not all. He was the one who called me about the five grand."

"I never liked him," the big man said. He was munching an Egg McMuffin I'd brought him. In fact, I'd brought him three.

We were standing in the Don's room, talking across his bed. He was still out.

The cop outside the door was gone. Benny said the detectives asked him to call when the Don could talk and they'd come by for a statement.

"There's some stuff happening, Benny," I said. "Let's sit down and talk about it."

We pulled two chairs together and sat at the foot of the Don's bed.

"What was Carlo up to?" Benny asked.

"He said you told him to drive me to deliver the five grand."

"I never did."

"I know. He did that himself. I figured out it was him, and we made the exchange."

"What was he sellin'?"

"He told me the Don got a phone call the day he was shot."

"The Don gets a lot of phone calls."

"Well, he got this one while Carlo was in the room. He told Carlo to leave, that he was walkin' to the restaurant."

"So what's that mean?"

"I don't know, but I had Carlo drive me to the Barge and let me in."

"How'd he do that? He ain't got no key."

"Yeah, he did. He said the Don gave him one to carry because he was startin' to forget his."

Benny frowned.

"Why didn't he tell me that?"

"Because the old man doesn't want you to know he's gettin' forgetful."

Benny shook his head and said, "Stupid," then looked at the Don quickly, checking to see if he'd heard him. "So what'd you find?"

"I went through the Don's desk and found a bunch of scribbled notes."

"What'd they say?"

"I don't know. There was too many to read right there and then, so I took them with me. When we got outside, somebody put one in Carlo's heart."

"One shot? From where?"

"I don't know," I said. "A ways off."

"A pro," Benny said. "Only a pro would be that good at night. Probably had an infrared scope."

"Why not plug me, too?"

"If he was a pro working on a contract he wouldn't," Benny said. "He's only gettin' paid for one."

I looked at the old man in the bed.

"They could be comin' for him next," I said.

"They gotta come through me to get him," Benny said.

"They might do that," I said. "You need somebody you can trust here with you."

"You're the only one I trust, Nicky."

"I can't stay here with you, Ben. But I can make a call and get somebody."

"Who?"

"Friend of mine," I said. "Maybe two. You can trust them."

"If you say so, Nicky."

"Okay," I said. "Let me make the calls, and then I'll get back to you. Have somebody here by this afternoon."

"Okay. You hear from Winky?"

"No. I'll go and check those addresses you gave me, askin' about him. And I've got to go through the Don's notes."

"Leave 'em with me," Benny said. "I'll go through 'em."

I hesitated.

"What?" he asked. "You think I ain't smart enough to find somethin'?"

"I think you're plenty smart, Benny," I said. "It's a good idea, because I'm gonna be on the move for a while. I'll go down to my car and get 'em. Oh, speakin' of the car." I took Carlo's keys out of my pocket. "Here's the keys to the limo, and whatever other keys Carlo had."

Benny took them. "These are for the limo, this one for the front door of the Barge. The rest must be his private keys."

"I'll be right back."

I went down to the car and got the envelope with the notes. Benny wasn't the sharpest knife in the drawer, but he knew the Don, and he could read his handwriting. If there was something there to find, he'd find it.

I brought it back up to the room and handed it to him.

"You went through the Don's drawer," he said.

"Yeah."

"He won't like that."

"Maybe," I said, "we won't have to tell him."

He looked at me for a few moments, then said, "Yeah, maybe."

"I'll call you about who I'm sendin' to back you up, Benny. You'll be able to trust them."

"Okay, Nicky," he said. He held up the envelope. "I'll start readin'."

"Let me know what you find out."

Thirty-Five

I WENT BACK TO MY PLACE AND USED THE PHONE TO MAKE ARRANGEMENTS
to back Benny up at the hospital. I called two P.I. buddies I know, Miles
Jacoby and Henry Po, and asked them each if they'd do it.

"Cash money?" Jacoby asked.

"A payin' gig, Jack," I said.

"I'll take the Don's money, Nick, but not yours," he said.

"That can be arranged."

Hank Po said the same thing. The three of us used to hire out to
each other for special jobs, but as we became friends we did it more as
a favor. But there was risk, here, and I wanted them to be compensated.
So the Don would pay them both.

I called Benny and told him to expect Jacoby and Po at the hospital.

"I ain't found nothin' in these notes yet, Nick," he said.

"Keep lookin', Benny."

With that taken care of I was ready to go looking for Benny's
contact, Winky. Benny had given me two addresses in Brooklyn. I
grabbed my windbreaker, hanging heavy with my gun in the pocket,
and my keys and headed for the door. When I opened it to step out I
ran into a brick wall.

Otherwise known as Tony Mitts.

As I bounced off him he advanced on me and grabbed me with both
hands.

"What the fuck, Nick?" he shouted. "What the fuck?"

He started to shake me, his eyes blazing with rage. My toes were barely touching the floor.

"Let me go, Tony."

"What the—"

"Don't make me shoot you."

He stopped short. I put my hand in my pocket, then pressed the barrel of my gun to his belly. His eyes cleared a bit as he felt the metal.

"Nick—"

"Let me go and calm down," I said. "Then we can talk."

Slowly, he released the front of my shirt and my feet touched down. I backed away, took my hand out of my pocket.

"I'm sorry," I said to him. "I'm all involved in my dad's death and I let the business about the rape slip."

"Jesus, Nick, what rape?" he asked. Now he looked anguished rather than enraged.

"Mary Ann told her sister that years ago she was raped."

"Years?"

"Two years, before you were engaged."

"That's before we started goin' out again."

"There's even some question as to whether or not it was rape," I said.

"If Mary Ann said it was rape, then it was." He clenched his big mitts into fists. "Did she go to the police?"

"She didn't."

"Who was it, Nick?"

"I'm not tellin' you that, Tony, because you'd go out and commit murder. That wouldn't help anyone."

"So he gets away with it?"

"Well . . . she forgave him, Tony."

"So it was somebody she knew?"

"I didn't say that."

"Why else would she forgive him?"

"I don't know," I said. "I can't get the answers from her, Tony, she's dead."

"Then I'll go ask Catherine," Tony said. "I'll wring her neck until she tells me."

"No you won't," I said. "you're gonna come with me now."

"Where?"

"I'm lookin' for a man named Winky. He might be able to tell me who shot my father. I need somebody to watch my back. If you help me, I'll help you. I'll keep working on Mary Ann's case and find out the truth, about the rape, and about her death. Deal?"

He stood there for a few moments, going over it in his head, and then said, "Deal."

"Let's go."

Tony had driven his car, but we left it parked in front of my building. It would be ticketed by the time we got back, but probably not towed. I didn't tell him that. No point in getting him even more upset.

The first place Benny told me to ask for Winky was a bar in Bay Ridge, on Eighty-Seventh Street and Fourth Avenue. It was about three doors down from an OTB office.

We parked down the street and walked to the bar. There were neon signs in the windows advertising "Budweiser" in red and "Heineken" in green. Above the door was printed "Rafe's."

Naturally, it was a dive, but I'd spent many a pleasant evening in dives. I felt at home in them.

The bar ran along one wall, almost the entire length of the place, which was impressive. Couldn't say that about the width of it, though. It was almost unable to accommodate Tony's wing span.

"This place stinks," he said.

"What kind of bars have you been hangin' out in?" I asked. "They all smell like this. It's a well-earned odor."

Beer, whiskey, sweat and despair. They had all soaked into the walls, and the grain of the wooden bar.

We went to the bar and added our elbows to the ones already leaning there. A few of the patrons gave us a look, but most of them were too busy nursing their beer.

"What'll it be?" the bartender asked. Or maybe he asked, "What'll ya have?" Either one sounded the same to me.

"Beer."

"What kind?"

"Whatever's on tap."

He drew two frothy mugs and set them down in front of us. Tony looked at his dubiously, and I wondered when he'd gotten so finicky. I picked mine up and took a sip. Pretty much made me finicky, too.

"I'm lookin' for Winky," I said to the bartender. "He been around, lately?"

"No."

"You sure?" I asked. "Benny told me I might find him here."

"Benny?"

"That's right."

The bartender squinted at me from beneath big, bushy black eyebrows that were shot through with gray. If he had any hair it would have been the same, but he was as bald as an egg.

"This about the Barracuda shootin'?"

"That's right," I said. "Benny told me I could find Winky here, or at a bar out on Pennsylvania Avenue."

"Naw, he don't go out there anymore," the bartender said. "He does his drinkin' here—when he's drinkin'."

"And when is that?"

"When he ain't gamblin'."

"And is that what he's doin' now?"

"Yup."

"Where?"

The bartender stroked the hard, black bristles on his cheeks and jaw.

"If I tell you, you'll let the Don know I helped?" he asked.

"I'll tell 'im."

"You can find him down the street."

"OTB?"

"That's right. As long as they're runnin', or they're open. Then he'll come back here until his poker game starts."

"What's he looks like."

"Tall, thin. Looks like he could use a good meal. But . . . you'll know him when you see him."

"Okay, thanks."

"If I was you I'd wait till he comes back here, then buy him a drink," the bartender said. "That'll make him more talkative."

"I don't have the time to waste."

"He ain't gonna be happy to be interrupted when he's playin' the horses."

"I'll have to take that chance," I said. "Thanks for the info."

I walked out of the bar with Tony behind me.

Thirty-Six

JUST THE SHORT TIME WE'D SPENT IN RAFE'S MADE THE SUN OUTSIDE SEEM ten times brighter.

"Now what?" Tony asked.

"OTB."

"We gonna interrupt the guy?"

"Oh, yeah."

"You know anythin' about him?"

"Like what?"

"Like how big he is?" Tony asked. "Or if he carries a gun?"

"No," I said, "but you're plenty big, and I carry a gun."

"I ain't fought much since high school, Nick."

I looked him up and down.

"But you kept in shape."

"So?"

"Just stand behind me," I said, "and look mean. You can do that, can't you?"

"Sure," he said. "I can do that."

We entered the OTB and went unnoticed. That's because there was a race going on, showing on the monitors around the place. All eyes were on the race and half the place was shouting while the other half—the half that was probably already out of the race—were watching in silence.

The loud one were yelling things like "Oh, come on!" or "Get up, get up, get up!", and the horse player's lament, "One time! One time!" They were either punching the air, pounding the back of the person next to them, or snapping their fingers.

But they all had one thing in common. They were all standing with their heads at the same angle, chins up, watching the monitors which were bolted to the ceiling. There was very little elbow room in the place.

Tony and I were the only ones not looking at the race. We were checking everybody out, looking for a tall, thin, hungry-looking race fan. Ultimately, we didn't find him until it was over and everybody's chins came down.

"There he is," I said.

"Where?"

"Black hair, dirty white T-shirt . . . and that blink."

That was why they called him "Winky." He had one eye that was constantly blinking, so he looked like he was always winking.

I knew there were horseplayers—real degenerates—who sold their blood for money they could bet with, and that's what Winky looked like.

"Now what?" Tony asked.

"Let's get him out of here before the next race," I said.

We approached him, and I signaled Tony to move to his other side.

"Winky!" I said. "Good to see ya. How're you doin' with the nags?"

"Huh?" He looked at me, frowned, his right eye going wink-wink-wink. "I know you?"

"Sure, you do," I said. "Nick Delvecchio. I'm friends with Benny Carbone."

"Benny?" Winky turned his head and looked at Tony, who did his best to appear menacing.

"Didn't you hear he was lookin' for you?" I asked.

"Uh, I might've, but I been on a hot streak."

"Let's step outside for a few minutes."

"I got a longshot in the next race," Winky complained.

"The quicker we make this, the quicker you'll get back in to play it."

I looked at Tony, and he got my message. He grabbed Winky's upper arm and squeezed.

"Yeah, yeah, okay," Winky said. "He don't hafta mangle me."

I nodded to Tony, who released the arm. We walked outside.

"Okay, whataya want?"

"What do you know about the Don's shooting?" I asked.

"What makes ya think I know anythin'?" he asked.

"Benny says you keep your ear to the ground," I said. "He says you're his friend and he can usually count on you."

"Yeah," Winky said. "Benny's my friend."

Which meant that I wasn't. Big surprise. I already knew that.

"Come on, Winky," I said. "Who put the hit out on the Don?"

"Like I know?"

"If you knew would you tell me?"

"If I knew I'd sell you the info."

"Would you sell it to Benny?"

He paused, then said, "Benny scares me, but yeah, because he'd pay me."

"Then he will pay you."

"Look," he said. "I don't know who put the hit out, but I'll try to find out. Gimme your number."

I gave him one of my cards.

"One more thing," I said.

"What?"

"Somebody shot Carlo, who drives the Don, last night," I said. "I was with him, but there was one shot and it hit him in the heart."

"A pro," Winky said.

"That's right. And how many pros would be working the city at one time? Last night whoever he was used a rifle. The shooting of the Don and my dad was done with an Uzi."

"Uzi?" Winky frowned. "That don't make sense. That sounds like the Jamaicans or South Americans."

"I know," I said. "That's what I was thinkin'."

"Those fuckers are crazy," Winky said.

"Then you better make sure they don't hear about you," I said.

"Yeah, uh, yeah," Winky said, rubbing his nose vigorously with the palm of his hand. "Look I gotta make this bet, and it'd be better if I had, uh, more money."

"What's the name of the horse?" I asked.

"Aroma Girl. She's been beaten fifty lengths in her last two races, but they're puttin' her on turf today. I been waitin' for this one."

I took out my wallet. I had two fifties, a ten and some singles. I took out the two fifties.

"One is for you," I said. "Put the other one on the horse to win, for me."

"Uh, okay, sure."

"Hey, I'll get in on that," Tony said. "Put twenty on the nose for me."

Winky took the twenty and stared at Tony. Mitts finally took out another twenty and handed it to him.

"We'll collect next time we see you," I said. "Where's it running?"

"Third at Belmont."

"Okay," I said. "Remember, call me as soon as you know anything."

"Yeah, okay. Oh, hey."

"What?"

"The other guy with the Don. That was your dad?"

"Yeah," I said. "They were friends. The Don is actually my Godfather."

"Sorry about your old man," Winky said. "I'll find out what I can."

"Thanks."

Thirty-Seven

WE WALKED BACK TO MY CAR.

"So that's what you do every day?" Tony asked, as we got inside.

"What?"

"Pay for information. Or scare it outta people. And then wait?"

"Not every day, Tony," I said, "but yeah, a lot of waiting."

"Now what?" he asked.

"Now I'll keep my word," I said. "You helped me out, so now we go and talk to Mary Ann's mother and sister again."

"Okay."

"And on the way, Tony," I said, glancing at him, "you can talk to me again."

"About what?"

"About everything, Tony," I said, turning the key. "About everything."

We were closer to the Grosso house than to my place, so we still left Tony's car where it was, on Sackett Street.

I used part of the drive to get my head back into the case. I went over my visit to Sal, our talk about the rape. I remembered I'd left his house believing him about two things. He didn't think it was rape, and he didn't kill her.

"Tony, if you want me to help you, you'll have to tell me the truth," I said.

"About what?"

"You and Mary Ann were engaged, right?"

"Right."

"And she never told you she was raped?"

"She never said a word to me, Nick," he said. "I swear."

"Why not, Tony?"

"I—I don't know," he said. "Maybe for the same reason you weren't gonna tell me."

"Because you'd kill the guy?"

"Yeah."

Tony was always a big baby to me. Women called him a teddy bear. If he ever hurt anybody it would have been by accident. But in my office his eyes had been filled with enough rage to kill.

"You don't believe me?" he asked.

"No, I do," I said. "I don't think you can fake the shock you showed when I told you. You're not that good an actor."

We drove in silence for a while, then Tony asked, "What did you mean there was a question whether it was a rape or not?"

"Mary Ann said it was, but the guy said it wasn't."

"And you believed him?"

"Yeah, I did."

"Why?"

"He was convincing," I said, "and it's very easy for a girl to yell rape."

"Easy?"

"Don't get me wrong," I said. "A woman has a right to say no, and lots of them get raped, but there are those who misuse the word."

"And you think Mary Ann was one of those?"

"I don't know," I said. "Let's see if we can find out."

Thirty-Eight

I PARKED IN FRONT OF ANGELA GROSSO'S HOUSE AND WE GOT OUT.

"What are you gonna do?" Tony asked, facing me across the top of my car.

"I'm gonna do what I do," I said. "Ask questions. Seems to me somebody has to know what the hell was goin' on with Mary Ann. Somebody has to know who the real Mary Ann was."

"Yeah," Tony said, "I did."

"I don't think so, Tony. I don't think you did."

"Who then?"

"Her mother?" I asked.

Tony shook his head.

"She didn't get along that good with her mother."

"Then how about her sister?" I asked. "After all, it was Catherine she told about the rape."

"What if there wasn't any rape?" Tony asked. "What if Catherine lied?"

"And why would she do that?"

Tony shrugged. "Maybe she was jealous of Mary Ann."

"Well, why don't we go inside and find out," I said.

We went up the walk to the front door and rang the bell. After a few moments I rang it again.

"Catherine might be at work," Tony said. "I don't know if she was ready to go back."

"Where else might she be?"

Tony shrugged.

"Where does she work?"

"The Brooklyn Museum."

"And her mother?"

"I don't know where she might be. Maybe the cemetery."

"Okay," I said. "I might as well take you back to your car."

"Museum's on the way," Tony said.

"Depending on how we go," I said.

The Museum was on Eastern Parkway, and we could have gone that way, but I didn't want him with me when I talked to Catherine again. So I jumped on the Belt Parkway and took that to downtown Brooklyn.

"Whataya want me to do now?" Tony asked when I dropped him by his car.

"Nothing," I said. "Just stay out of it. I don't want you to lose your head and do somethin' stupid."

"You're gonna tell me everythin', right?" he asked.

"I'll tell you whatever I find out," I promised.

I drove away, leaving him standing there. I took Flatbush Avenue to Grand Army Plaza, drove around it and veered off onto Eastern Parkway. It might have been a good day to turn into Prospect Park, but I didn't have the time.

There was a Grand Army Plaza in Manhattan, too, across from the Plaza Hotel. I always wondered why nobody had the imagination to come up with another name.

The Museum had on-premise parking, so I didn't have to go looking for a space on the street. The shittiest man who ever lived invented parking meters. If I didn't have to use one, that suited me.

I entered the Museum. The day was about ten degrees hotter than usual, which put it in the mid to high 80s. The chill of the Museum air-conditioning was welcome.

I stopped at the first rent-a-cop I saw—staring off into space—and asked him for Catherine Grosso.

"She works in the office," he said, and directed me.

"You mind tellin' me what her job is?"

The guard shrugged and said, "I think she's a secretary or somethin'."

He was probably a retired cop just playin' out the string.

"Thanks."

He nodded, went back to staring.

●

I MADE my way up some marble steps to the second floor, found a string of offices. Catherine was sitting at a desk in the third one.

"Catherine."

Her head jerked up and she frowned when she saw me standing in the doorway. She was wearing a pair of wire-rimmed glasses, took them off so she could see me better.

"Nick? What are you doin' here?"

"I needed to talk to you," I said. "I tried your house, and then Tony told me where you worked."

"Tony told you?"

"Your mother wasn't home."

"She—she's probably at the cemetery."

"Can we walk and talk?" I asked.

"Oh, sure. Just wait for me out in the hall."

I nodded, and stepped out.

Thirty-Nine

SHE JOINED ME AFTER A FEW MOMENTS. SHE HAD HER GLASSES IN HER
hand, kept them folded there.

"You get somebody to cover for you?" I asked.

"For a few minutes."

"Are you important here?"

She laughed.

"Oh, no," she said. "I'm just an assistant."

"To who?"

She shrugged.

"To a lot of people. I'm hoping for a promotion, soon."

"I'm sure you'll get it," I said.

"I hope you're right," she said. "What was it you wanted to talk
about?"

"Well, if it's okay, I'd like to talk about Mary Ann, and the rape."

"Oh, that." She folded her arms, hugging herself. "Did you talk to Sal?"

"I did," I said. "He says it wasn't rape. He said he and Mary Ann
had a relationship."

"They never—"

"Oh, not a sexual one," I said. "He just said they were friends."

She didn't reply.

"Does that sound like Mary Ann to you, Catherine?" I asked. "Did
she make friends with men?"

"Mary Ann—" she said, then stopped short. "Nick, Mary Ann wasn't what everybody thought she was."

"And what was that, Catherine?" I asked. "What did everybody think she was?"

She hesitated. "A good girl."

I'd heard the talk in high school, the talk that Tony had chosen not to believe. I never took steps to find out if it was true or not. I wasn't friends with the guys who claimed to have been with her.

"Are you talkin' about high school?" I asked. "Or are we not goin' back that far?"

"Yes," she said, "high school—and after."

"And how about when she went away?"

Catherine shrugged and hugged herself tighter. "I only know that when she came back she was different. Something had changed her."

"And that was before Sal?"

"Yes."

"So, changed her how?"

"Well, all of a sudden she didn't even like to talk about sex," Catherine said. "It was as if she'd taken a pledge or somethin'."

"So she was off sex after being promiscuous for . . . what? Years?"

"I guess."

"And did your mother know about Mary Ann's promiscuity?"

"Oh, yes, she knew," Catherine said, "but she went on pretending that Mary Ann was this saint, you know? She couldn't face the truth."

"And what about you? Could you face the truth?"

"Me? What did I care? It didn't matter to me if she slept around or not."

"Come on, Catherine," I said. "You were the younger sister. Weren't you jealous? Weren't you angry about the way your mother treated Mary Ann, ignoring the fact that she was a slut?"

"I didn't say that!" Catherine said, loudly. So loudly that it echoed. She looked around quickly, then pulled me down on a nearby bench.

"I didn't say she was a slut," she said.

"Did you ever hear your mother say that?"

She squirmed.

"Catherine?"

"I heard them having an argument," she said. "During it my mother did call her a slut, but Mary Ann told her that was all over now. She said she was going to marry Tony. My mother told her to make sure Tony never found out about her past."

"And what did Mary Ann say to that advice?"

"She said she was gonna tell Tony everythin'," Catherine said, "That they could only have a good marriage if they were honest with each other."

"What did your mother think of that?"

"She thought Mary Ann was bein' foolish. She even said she was crazy. There was no way Tony would still marry her if she told him. Mary Ann said he would, that Tony loved her no matter what."

"Then what?"

"That was it. Mary Ann left the room. I . . . hid."

"Did you and your mother ever talk about the argument?"

"No."

"When did it happen?"

"The day before."

"The day before what?" I asked, to be clear. "The reunion?"

"N-no," Catherine said. "The day before Mary Ann died."

I asked a few more questions while I walked her back to her office.

"Catherine, did Mary Ann have trouble sleeping?"

"No. She slept like a baby." She sounded almost envious.

"But she died of an overdose of sleeping pills. They were your mother's How did she get them?"

"I—I didn't give them to her. If they were my mother's they were in her bathroom. We were never allowed in mother's bathroom. Never!"

Some aspects of childhood—like certain rules—died hard.

"I'm not accusin' you of anything," I said. "I'm just tryin' to get some answers."

Before we got to the door I turned and took her by the shoulders.

"I don't think Mary Ann ever told Tony anything, Catherine," I said. "I've spoken to him a couple of times. I let it slip about the rape and he exploded."

"Did you tell him who did it?"

"No," I said. "I don't want him to know."

"So is Sal gonna get away with rape?"

"I'm not convinced it as rape," I said.

"But Mary Ann said—"

"Maybe she convinced herself it was," I said. "You said she took the pledge. Maybe she was ashamed . . . Sal didn't act like a rapist, Catherine. He acted like he was in love with Mary Ann."

Catherine bit her lip and asked, "Weren't they all?"

Forty

I KEPT MY ANSWER TO MYSELF UNTIL I GOT BACK TO MY CAR.

No, I wasn't in love with Mary Ann Grosso, and good for me. I had enough problems without being part of that club. But with Tony and Sal as members, I wondered how many others there were? What about Sammy? And Joey the Nose?

But despite what Catherine told me, I could hear in her voice that she was envious or jealous of her older sister. Was she still jealous of Mary Ann, even after her death? And would she say anything to Tony about his Mary Ann not being so perfect?

And what about their mother, Angela? What did she know that she was keeping to herself?

I was going to have to talk to my old school buddies, and to Mary Ann's mother again, but first I had to check in with Benny on the Don's condition.

I went back to my office to use the phone. Mobile phones were getting to be all the rage, but they were expensive and I didn't think they'd last. Who needed them with pay phones on every corner? And I was very happy with the phone on my desk.

Now, if I could figure out a way to exist without the damn answering machine. Once again as I entered it was winking its red eye at me.

I sat behind my desk and stared at the machine. I really toyed with the idea of not listening to the messages. However, if I did that I'd end up sitting in my office alone, thinking about . . . things. Things like how the man who raised me wasn't actually my father. And if he wasn't, who was?

I pressed the play button.

First it was Maria: "Nick, call me at Pop's. I need to know when to schedule the funeral."

Next, Father Vinnie: "Nick, we need to hear from you. We want to know what's going on."

The third was a surprise: "Mr. Delvecchio, this is Detective Del Costa. Please give me a call at my office. I need to, um, I would like to talk to you about something."

The fourth, fifth and sixth calls were from Benny: "Nick, the Don is awake. He's askin' for ya."

I ignored all the other messages, left the office and headed for the hospital.

Forty-One

WHEN I GOT TO THE HOSPITAL PO AND JACOBY WERE OUTSIDE THE DOOR.

"Who kicked you out?" I asked.

"The Don woke up and got agitated because he didn't know us," Jacoby said.

"We thought it was better if we stepped out," Po said.

Jacoby had been a middleweight boxer in his youth and still looked in shape. Hank Po and I could also have been middleweights at some time. When the three of us were together it could have looked like we were created by the same person.

"Thanks. I'll see what I can do."

"It's okay," Hank said. "We're probably better off out here, anyway."

"Benny?"

"He's real protective of the Don," Jack said. "I'd hate to be in the ring with him. He's a big guy."

"But with us out here," Po said, "nobody's gonna get inside."

"Good," I said. "Benny call the cops yet, about the Don bein' awake?"

"Not yet," Po said. "We all agreed you should talk to him first."

"Okay, thanks." I went inside.

Benny turned quickly, his hand going inside his jacket. He relaxed when he saw it was me.

"I told you that you could trust those guys, Benny," I said.

"I only trust you, Nick," he said, "and so does the Don."

I looked down at the bed and the old man looked back at me. He had blue eyes, clear as could be, and he smiled at me.

"Ciao, Nicholas."

"Uncle."

I usually called him "Mr. Barracondi." Once I wasn't a kid anymore "Godfather" seemed dramatic. Thank you Mr. Puzo.

"How are you feelin'?" I asked.

"Worn out," he said. "Shot up. I am sorry about your Papa."

"I know," I said. "What did you see, Uncle?"

"What did I see?" he asked. "I am an old man, with old eyes. I saw nothing. What I heard, that is different. I heard the chatter of the gun. Boom-boom-boom-boom. Glass everywhere. And blood. Your Papa, he pushed me down. Probably why he is dead and I am alive."

"He's dead because he caught a few more bullets than you did," I said. "In worse places."

"Ah," he said, and a tear formed in his eye. "My oldest friend, you know?"

"Who were they, Uncle?" I asked. "Who killed Pop? And tried to kill you?"

"If I knew," he said, "I would tell you. And you and Benny would kill them."

"Uncle, the cops are lookin', I'm lookin', we've put the word out. If someone put a contract out on you we'll find out. But if you know—"

"A contract?" He laughed until he choked and Benny put his hand on the old man's chest until the coughing stopped.

"That was the old days," he rasped, then. "There was no contract. It was probably somebody with an old grudge."

"So who has a grudge?"

"Lots of people. Benny can make you a list."

I looked at Benny and he shrugged.

"Uncle, did Benny tell you that Carlo is dead?"

"Si."

"If it was a grudge why'd they kill Carlo?"

"I do not know. Maybe because they missed me, and now they can't get to me or Benny, so that was the only way. Too bad. Carlo was a good boy."

"Carlo told me you got a call before you went to Rizzo's," I said. "Who called?"

He closed his eyes.

"Ï don't remember."

"He said after the call you told him you'd walk to the restaurant. You don't walk anywhere, Uncle."

"I must've felt like a walk that day."

"Must have?"

"I told you, Nicholas, I don't remember." He closed his eyes again and turned his head away. "I am tired."

"Uncle, we have to call the detectives and tell them you're awake."

"So call them."

"If you have somethin' you want to tell us before they get here, you have to do it now."

He didn't respond. I looked at Benny and he shrugged again.

"Okay," I said.

I started away and the Don said, "Nicholas."

"Yes, Uncle?"

He turned his head and looked at me.

"Those two boys, you brought them?"

"Yes."

"You trust them?"

"With my life."

"They would die for you?"

"Yes," I said, although I wasn't sure.

"Would they die for me?"

Before I could answer he drifted off again.

Forty-Two

I PULLED BENNY OVER TO THE DOOR WITH ME.

"Why's he lyin', Ben?"

"The Don don't lie, Nicky."

"Yeah, he does," I said. "And he is."

"Nick, don't say that."

I could see that if I argued further I'd be banging my head against a stone wall. I'd also risk getting Benny really angry with me. I moved on.

"Ben, you're gonna have to call the detectives," I said, "and don't tell them I was here."

"Okay. Which one should I call?"

"Did they both leave you cards?"

"Yes."

"Call the sergeant, Hicks," I said.

"Okay, Nick."

"Just give me twenty minutes to get out of here."

Benny nodded.

I stepped outside.

"Anythin'?" Jacoby asked.

"The Don's lying to me."

"Why?"

"I don't know."

"What'd he say?" Po asked.

"He doesn't know who fired the shots," I said. "He rejects the idea that it might be a contract. Instead he said it was probably somebody with a grudge, but he didn't give me any names."

"Could he still be . . . confused?" Po asked.

"In shock?" Jacoby said.

"I don't think so," I said. "I think he knows exactly what he's doin'. I just have to figure out what the hell it is."

"And what about Benny?" Hank Po asked.

"When I suggested the Don was lyin' he got mad."

"He's incredibly loyal, isn't he?" Jacoby asked.

"Yes, he is. Sometimes it's scary."

"Sometimes?" Po asked.

"You guys better stay out here," I said. "I told Benny to call Sergeant Hicks. He and Detective Del Costa will probably be here soon."

"Okay," Po said. "What do we tell them when they ask us why we're here?"

"Tell the truth," I said. "You're bein' paid."

"What if they ask by who?" Jacoby asked.

"Don't tell 'em unless you have to."

"And if we have to?"

I took a breath. They couldn't say the Don was paying them. He was out of it. Benny? I don't think they'd believe he was smart enough.

"Okay," I said, "tell 'em you work for me."

They nodded.

"What are you gonna do now?" Jack asked.

"I've got to find out what the Don is lyin' about," I said, "and why."

I made sure I got away from the hospital before Hicks arrived. And since Del Costa would probably be with Hicks, I'd have to put off calling her until later.

That meant I had to go to Pop's house to see Maria and Vinnie.

When I got to Pop's I let myself in. There were cars out front, and lots of people in the living room.

Great.

Maria spotted me and came rushing over.

"What's goin' on?" I asked.

"When the neighborhood heard that Pop was dead they just . . . started turning up."

"How are you feedin' all of them? Gettin' them stuff to drink?"

"They're showin' up with food and drinks, Nick," she said. "I can't believe it. Wait, here's Mrs. Trombetta. Vinnie's in the kitchen."

Some of the people I knew and exchanged greetings with on the way to the kitchen. Other people I had no clue who they were.

In the kitchen Vinnie was standing at the sink, talking to a man and a woman. When he saw me he excused himself, came over and slapped a bottle of Rolling Rock into my hand.

"They even knew Pop's brand," he said.

"This is weird."

"I know. A wake without a body. Do you know when we'll be able to—"

"Not for a while, Vinnie. There's still an investigation goin' on. The detectives are still waitin' to talk to the Don."

"How is he? When's that gonna happen?"

"He woke up today. The detectives are probably talkin' to him now."

"Did you talk to him?"

"He told Benny he wanted to see me," I said. "I spoke to him before the cops, but he didn't tell me anything. Claims he didn't see anything, and doesn't know anything."

"What's he say about Pop?"

"That he saved his life," I answered. "He says Pop pulled him to the ground. It's probably why Pop took more bullets than the Don did."

"Pop's a hero."

"A dead hero, Vinnie."

"Nick—"

"Well, you can be proud of him," I went on. "Apparently he's your dad, not mine."

"Nick," Vinnie said, putting his hand on my shoulder. He was wearing an open neck polo shirt, no collar, but his manner was still that of a priest. "Blood tests can be wrong. We can do it all again after this is over."

"Sure," I said. "Look, I'm sorry. Really, I haven't even been thinkin' about that. All I've been thinkin' about is findin' out who the shooters were."

"What about the thing with Mary Ann Grosso? You told her mother you'd look into it."

"And I am," I said, "when I have the time. I talked to both Tony and Catherine today."

"Catherine?"

"Mary Ann's sister."

"Oh, yeah. I was out of high school when she came in. Maybe I should pay her mother a visit? In my official capacity, I mean."

"Sure, Father Vinnie," I said. "Maybe she'd like that."

"Father?" someone said, coming over.

"Oh, hi," he said. "This is my brother Nick. Nick, Mr. Voulo, Pop's neighbor."

"Your dad was a very nice man," Voulo said. He was tall, gray haired, and well-tanned, and I didn't remember ever having seen him in the neighborhood.

"Where do you live?"

"Two doors down," he said. "My wife and I moved in last year. Your dad was very welcoming." He looked at Vinnie. "We have to leave, Father."

"I'll come and say goodbye to your wife. Nick?"

"Go ahead, Vin," I said. "I'll stay here and finish this."

He nodded, took Voulo out of the kitchen.

I was thinking the house was full of people, a lot of whom I didn't know. How was I to know there wasn't a shooter in there, somewhere?

Forty-Three

WAS I BEING PARANOID?

Hell, somebody had shot my old man. Maybe they were after the Don, but they'd managed to kill Vito Delvecchio. Who was to say there wasn't somebody here in the house . . . nah, I was being paranoid. Whoever had killed Pop—the Mafia, the Russians, the Jamaicans— what reason could they have for putting somebody in Pop's house? None at all. They'd be concentrating on getting to the Don, again.

Maria came into the kitchen with a tray of food.

"Mrs. Delgado made lasagna."

"Good," I said. "Save it for us for later, when everybody leaves."

She giggled, and said, "Help me make room in the fridge."

There were already a bunch of plates and Tupperware in there, but we managed to shove the lasagna in. I knew Mrs. Delgado from the neighborhood and knew she could cook. For a Spanish woman she made a hell of a lasagna.

Maria pushed it all the way in the back, then covered it. When she came out of the fridge she grinned at me and said, "Our secret."

Then she started to cry.

When the crowd thinned out Maria, Father Vinnie and I got the kitchen to ourselves.

"What's goin' on, Nick?" Maria asked.

I gave her a quick rundown so she knew what Vinnie knew, then filled in some blanks. Finally, I told them what I thought I was going to have to do.

"But why would Uncle Dom lie?" Maria asked, for the third time.

"That's what I have to find out, Maria," I said. "I'm at a disadvantage until I do."

"What about the shooter?" Father Vinnie asked.

"Shooter?" I asked. "You gettin' the lingo down, Father?"

"Get stuffed," Vinnie said. "Do you think the same people who shot Pop and the Don shot at you? And killed Carlo?"

"I'm not sure they were shootin' at me," I said. "They killed Carlo clean, with one shot. Also, the people who killed Pop fired off I don't know how many rounds. Maybe hundreds."

"So, two different . . . shooters?" Maria asked.

"See what you started?" I said to Vinnie. "Look, guys, I can't stop what I'm doin' to check in with you."

"We're worried about you," Vinnie said.

"When's the last time you slept?"

I had probably gotten three hours since the first shooting.

"I've slept."

"For how long?" she asked.

"Don't worry about me," I said.

"Can you just call in from time to time so we know you're alive?" Vinnie asked.

"Why don't you just pray for me to stay alive? Then you won't have to worry."

"Nick!" Maria said.

"Sorry, Vinnie," I said. "I didn't mean —"

"Don't worry about it, Nick," he said. "Where are you headin' after here?"

"Believe it or not," I said, "I have a date with a lady detective."

"A date?" Maria asked.

"Well . . . sort of . . ."

Forty-Four

I LEFT THE HOUSE WITHOUT CALLING DETECTIVE DEL COSTA. I FIGURED she'd still be at the hospital trying to get something out of the Don that I couldn't get. I doubted he'd give it to them. He'd use that "I'm tired" excuse on them, too.

It was getting dark. Since I had nowhere else to go at the moment, I drove back to my place.

I stopped at Sam's door and knocked. When she opened it she smiled. Her door was the only one I felt I could always knock on and find a smile.

"You look tired. Hungry, too?"

"I am," I said. "I was supposed to have some lasagna, but it didn't work out." When I left the house a new group of people were just arriving. Maria and I would have to break into our private stash another time.

"Come on in," she said. "I have some leftovers."

"Take out?" I asked, closing her door behind me.

"Home-cooked."

"Good."

Her apartment was like mine, minus the office.

"Here." Her arm came out of the kitchen door clutching a beer. I grabbed it. A cold Killian's Red, the top already popped. I carried it over to her desk, took a peek at the computer screen. It was black, even though the power was on. I studied the keyboard, saw a key marked SLEEP MODE.

"What's been happening?" she asked. "Come on into the kitchen and tell me."

I went in, sipped my beer and told her everything I had told my brother and sister while she heated up some leftover chicken and potatoes.

I finished my story at the table while I ate and washed it down with a second beer.

"When are you going to call the lady detective?" she asked.

"When I get back to my desk."

"What do you think she wants?"

"I don't know," I said. "Maybe an exchange of information."

"Why would she be that cooperative?"

"I don't know," I said. "Maybe she's got a crush on me."

"Well, you said she was good looking."

"I said she was hot."

"Oh, yeah."

"How's your book goin'?"

"Changing the subject?"

"Oh, yeah."

She grinned.

"It's goin' fine. Nick."

"Yes?"

"Okay if I go and see your sister tomorrow?" she asked. "Maybe she needs somebody to talk to. You said she was upset today."

"She's got Father Vinnie."

"That's a man."

"A priest."

"Her brother," she said. "She probably needs a woman to talk to."

"Then maybe it's a good idea," I said. "Thanks, Sam."

"I just want to help."

"This was really good," I said, pushing the empty plate away. "Thanks."

I stood up. She walked me to the door. I took the rest of my second beer with me.

"I'll go see Maria after breakfast," she said. "Ham and eggs?"

"If I'm around," I said. "Gimme a knock in the mornin'."

Forty-Five

ALONE IN MY OFFICE I ONCE AGAIN THOUGHT BACK TO THE QUESTION of the blood tests. What was I supposed to do with the fact that my whole heritage—or lineage—was a lie? The answer was, at the present time, nothing. There were other things going on that were more important, such as people's lives. I could cry about my own problems later.

I checked my watch. If the Don was as unresponsive to the cops as he was to me, Detective Del Costa might be at her desk. I dialed the precinct and asked for her. Moments later, she picked up.

"Del Costa, Squad."

"You get anythin' out of the Don?" I asked.

"No," she said. "Did you?"

I remained silent.

"Come on," she said, "I know Big Benny called you first."

"I got nothin'," I said. "He claims he doesn't remember anythin'."

"He's lying," she said.

"I know he is," I said, "the question is, why? And why lie to me?"

She hesitated, then said, "You're serious, aren't you?"

"Hell yeah," I said. "I've been waitin' for him to wake up because I was sure he'd tell me somethin' important."

"You think maybe he's trying to protect you?" she asked.

I paused, then said, "I didn't think of that."

"You are family, right?" she asked. "I mean, real family?"

"Yeah," I said, "sort of."

"So maybe he doesn't want you getting shot."

I got a cold, fluttery feeling in my stomach and tried to ignore it.

"So Detective," I said, "what was it you wanted me to call you about?"

"I just thought maybe you'd like to meet for a drink," she replied.

"Meet?" I asked. "Like . . . a date?"

"I was thinking more of an exchange of information."

"Sounds good," I said. "When?"

"Half an hour?"

"Where?"

"Why don't you pick," she said, "as long as it's not a cop bar."

Okay, so she didn't want to be seen with me. Probably didn't want word getting back to Hicks.

"Let's go someplace no self-respecting cop would ever go," I said.

"A coffee bar?"

"A singles bar," I said. "A place called Last Exit, on Atlantic Avenue."

"A singles bar?"

"During the day it's a neighborhood bar, at night it gets kind of trendy and caters to singles. No cops, though."

"Well," she said. "Atlantic Avenue is far enough away. Okay, I'll meet you there in half an hour."

"If you're hungry I'll order some appetizers."

"Suits me," she said. "See you there."

I hung up, stood up to leave, decided to change my clothes and maybe put on some cologne. If I was going to Last Exit I figured I might as well look like a single on the prowl.

Forty-Six

LAST EXIT WAS JUST DOWN THE BLOCK FROM PETE'S ALE HOUSE, BUT YOU were more likely to run into cops at Pete's because of their beer selection.

The front of Last Exit was not fancy. In fact, it kind of looked like a dive. Over the door was a neon sign that read "Last Exit" with a neon arrow pointing to the door. It was the kind of place you might see Pete Gunn walking into.

The bar was long, very shiny mahogany. The inside had a little more class than the outside had.

The singles were in full swing. It looked like an under-thirty crowd and I was starting to think I'd picked the wrong place. The bar was crowded, and so were most of the tables. Even if we got a table, talking might be a problem. Especially if we had to yell at each other about shooting and blood.

I found a place at the end of the bar nearest the door so I'd see Del Costa when she arrived.

I ordered a Brooklyn Lager, fended off the feelers put out by a couple of thirtyish singles who were probably as out of place as I was.

One of the ladies was just walking away from me when I saw Del Costa step inside the door.

I almost didn't recognize her. She was wearing dark blue jeans, a red belt and a maroon silk blouse. She wasn't big breasted but the silk hugged what she had, which was very nice indeed. It was air-conditioned inside Last Exit and the silk made it easy to see that she reacted to the chill. Her hair was different, too. She had pulled it back into a ponytail that was worn sort of high up. Her mass of black hair was pulled back so tightly it gave her face and head a whole different look. Very unbusinesslike.

"Breaking hearts?" she asked, as she approached me.

"I think they're desperate," I said.

"It's kind of crowded in here."

"There's a little courtyard in the back with tables and chairs," I said. "I haven't been out there to see if it's also full. Would you like a drink?"

"Beer's good," she said. "You live near here, right?"

"Oh, yeah, right. I do. I mean, I drove, I didn't walk, but yeah, I live on—"

"And you have beer in your fridge?"

"Um, sure."

"Then why don't we just go there?" she suggested. "I mean, it'll be a lot quieter."

I looked around while I tried to think of an answer. The guys were admiring her, probably wondering what she was doing with me.

Of course, if she walked out with me they'd all be crushed, wouldn't they?

"Sure," I said. "Let's go."

Losers! I thought as we walked out.

Forty-Seven

I HOPED SAM DIDN'T HEAR US COMING DOWN THE HALL. I MEAN, WE WERE just neighbors . . . well, no, we were friends, but not more than that . . . but still . . . I breathed a sigh of relief when we got inside and I locked the door behind Del Costa.

"Beer?" I asked.

"Sure."

"Bottle or glass?"

"Let's go with the bottle and see what happens," she said.

I went to the kitchen and came back with two opened bottles of Newcastle. Might as well break out the good stuff.

She had dropped her purse on the sofa and sat down next to it. Keeping her gun close, I thought, as I handed her the beer.

"Thanks."

I hadn't had time to notice in the bar, but her make-up was different. It seemed softer, and her lipstick was not as harsh a red as it had been the other times I'd seen her. She licked her lips and sipped from the bottle.

The way she smelled was also different. Less of a work scent and more of a . . . what? Play scent? Social?

The sofa had three cushions. I sat down and left the one between us empty.

"You look great tonight," I said. "Different."

"I don't get out much," she said. "I'm usually either dressed for work, or I'm at home in sweats."

I had a quick flash of her in sweats, then tried to push the thought away. There was something in the air, here, unless I was reading it wrong.

I sipped my beer and then asked, "What's on your mind, Detective?"

"We got back a complete report on ballistics," she said.

"And?"

"There's something there I thought you'd find interesting."

"And what was that?"

"Well, all of the rounds we found were fired from an Uzi—except one."

"One round different? What kind of gun was that from?" I asked.

"A sniper's rifle," she said. "A Dragunov SVD."

"A Russian gun?"

She nodded.

"Very popular in the seventies, very accurate from up to six hundred meters. I can give you all the specs if you like."

"I don't care about the specs," I said. "Uzis can be bought by anybody, but a Russian sniper rifle? Wouldn't that be a specialized weapon? You wouldn't see a bunch of Jamaicans buying a Russian sniper rifle from the trunk of a car, like they would an Uzi."

"You're right."

"So what the hell—some Russian sniper took a shot while somebody else was firing hundreds of rounds from an Uzi?"

"Maybe they were using the Uzi fire for cover. There's something else."

"What?"

"The same rifle was used to kill the driver, Carlo."

"Okay," I said, putting my bottle down so I could gesture with both hands while agitated. You can't take the Italian out of the boy. "So this connects both shootings. Somebody with a Russian rifle shot at Pop and the Don, and killed Carlo. The question is, was it somebody from the Russian *Mafiya*, or is it somebody trying to pin it on the Russians?"

"That's what I'm wondering."

"What's your partner wonderin'?"

"He's thinking a little differently than I am."

"Like how?"

"He's still looking into the first shooting as an attempt on the Don."

"And you?"

"I'm kinda wondering who might have had a reason to shoot your dad?"

"Nobody," I said.

"You sure?"

"I'm positive," I said. "Sure, my dad worked on the docks and he was a union rep for a long time, but he's been retired for years. He hasn't done anythin' to get shot over."

"So he was just in the wrong place at the wrong time?"

"That's what I was thinkin'."

"And that's what Hicks is thinking."

"But you're thinkin' different. Why?"

"Well," she said. "That's one of the reasons I called you."

"What?"

"The Russian 7.62 slug was found in your father."

Forty-Eight

I GRABBED MY BOTTLE AS I STOOD UP QUICKLY FROM THE SOFA. I TOOK A swig while I paced. I just felt the need to move.

"You're sayin' my father was the target?"

"*I'm* saying that," she was quick to point out. "Nobody else is. Hicks even has our boss convinced the Don was the target. The fact that his driver was also killed supports that."

"The Don said my father jumped up and dragged him to the ground, tryin' to save him," I pointed out. "Could the bullet have struck him then?"

"The bullet hit him in the heart," she said. "Dead center. Just like the driver. If it hit him by accident, but took him in the heart, that'd have to be a helluva coincidence."

"If Hicks is right," I said, "then the Don is still a target."

"Right."

"Are you covering the hospital?"

"We've got a couple of men watching it, but they're not in plain sight."

"So you're hoping to catch the killer in the act," I said. "You don't care if it's while he's killing the Don."

"Not me," she said.

"Okay, Hicks and your boss."

"Right."

"But if my Pop was the target, why kill Carlo?"

"Maybe they were trying to kill you," she said. "That'd make more sense."

"But we're talkin' about another heart shot," I said. "They couldn't have missed me and hit Carlo in the heart. We were a good six feet apart. That's not a miss."

"No. That's a good shot."

"Two good shots, straight to the heart. We're dealin' with a pro, a crack shot. A sniper."

"For hire, maybe," she said. "Not a member of the Italian Mafia, and not a member of the Russian Red *Mafiya*, or any other gang. A hired pro."

"With a fondness for Russian rifles?"

"That might still be a ploy to blame the Russians," she said.

I kept pacing. She got up and walked over to me. She put her hand on my arm.

"Stop. Stand still."

I did. She stood very close to me. In her heels she was about an inch taller than me.

"There's nothing we can do about this tonight," she said. "This was just something I felt I had to tell you."

"I appreciate it."

"I can't begin to understand how you feel about losing your father. Both my parents are still alive. But to lose him the way you did, and now this."

I laughed, shook my head.

"What?"

"You don't know the half of it."

"What do you mean?"

"It's not important—"

"Maybe it is," she said.

So I told her about the blood tests.

"Oh my God," she said. "With everything you have to deal with, you don't need that, too. What have you done about it?"

"Nothin'," I said. "I've been tryin' not to think about it so I can concentrate on everythin' else. Plus I'm workin' another case." I told her about Mary Ann Grosso's apparent suicide.

"And you're still working that?"

"I took the case on first," I said. "I feel an obligation . . ."

She shook her head.

"You must be going crazy right now," she said. "I should leave . . ."

But she didn't. Instead she leaned forward and kissed me on the mouth, a soft, tentative kiss.

"Too forward?" she asked.

"No, I'm just . . . surprised."

"Well . . . this is the other reason I called you."

"Are you serious?"

"I don't date cops, Nick," she said. "And I don't like going to bars and picking up men for one night stands—although I'm not proud to say, I have done it."

"And me?"

"I thought we had something . . . in common," she said. "The last time we talked I felt that you might be somebody I could . . . relax with."

"Detective Del Costa," I asked, "are you tellin' me this is a booty call?"

She grinned sheepishly and asked, "Would that be so bad?"

"No," I said, pulling her to me, "no, that wouldn't be so bad, at all."

Forty-Nine

I WOKE UP THE NEXT MORNING WITH A LADY COP IN BED WITH ME. THAT was a first.

Del Costa's first name was Lydia. She was lying on her side with her back to me and I had to admire the view. She had a very toned body that she kept that way with jogging and volley ball. Long, strong legs, a rounded, solid butt, mid-sized firm tits with brown nipples that were hidden from me now, but I had spent a lot of time on them during the night.

I tore my eyes from her body—did I say how smooth and creamy her skin was?—and stared at the ceiling. I thought about everything I had learned from her last night. She had kept me so busy during the night, so this was my first chance to go over it, but I found it was all too much and too early. I needed more diversion.

I reached out and stroked her buttocks, ran my middle finger along her butt crack. She must have been awake because she rolled toward me right away.

She smiled and said, "I was wondering how you'd feel about all this in the morning."

"Well, about all this," I said, running my hands over her, "I feel pretty damn lucky. About the other stuff? I haven't had time to process it, yet."

"Mmm," she said, putting her arms around my neck, "well, maybe I can keep you from having to do that, yet."

We came together but before anything could develop there was a knock on the front door.

"Oops," I said, suddenly remembering.

"Who's that so early?" she wondered aloud.

"My neighbor," I said. "Checkin' to see if I want breakfast."

More knocking.

"Your neighbor?"

I nodded.

"A girl?"

I nodded again.

"Does she make you breakfast often?"

"Sometimes," I said. "Last night she said she'd knock and see if I want breakfast this morning."

"And do you?"

"Well, yeah," I said, "but not right now."

"This neighbor," she said. "Is she a neighbor with benefits?"

"Not for a long time," I said. "Right now we're just friends."

"Uh-huh. I'm not stepping into the middle of anything, am I?"

"No, no," I said.

Knocking . . .

"But you're not going to answer the door, are you?" she asked.

"Ah, no."

"Because you don't want to have to explain?"

"Well," I said, looking down at our naked bodies, pressed up against each other, "I'm kinda comfortable, right now."

"You know," she said, "I'm not even gonna get involved in this. You'll just have to explain yourself later. Right now I want some attention."

"I have no problem with that," I said.

She pushed me onto my back so she could lie on top of me, trapping my hard cock between us. She rubbed her black pubic hair over me while we kissed and pretty soon had gotten so worked up she was getting me wet. Finally, she lifted her hips and just slid me into her, and then started working her butt up and down, biting her lip and squeezing her eyes shut. . . .

The knocking at the door stopped.

Fifty

LATER, I WATCHED HER GET UP AND TROT OVER TO THE BATHROOM TO take a shower. Her hair had come down from its ponytail pretty quick last night, and now was a mass of curls running down her back.

When I heard the shower go on I got up and pulled on a pair of boxer shorts. I took my terry cloth robe from the closet and laid it on the bed for her. Next, I went out to the kitchen and got a pot of coffee started. I really didn't have anything to make for breakfast, but then I wasn't all that sure she'd be staying.

I went to where we'd left our clothes on the floor and started picking them up. I felt bad about letting Sam knock on the door so long. It was true we had slept together in the past, and that we were more friends now than anything, but I still hadn't wanted to have to answer the door and make an excuse, and I certainly didn't want to have to explain anything to her later on.

I left our clothes on the sofa and went back to the kitchen. By the time she came in wearing the robe, her hair wet from the shower, the coffee was ready.

"That smells good," she said.

"I don't make the best coffee," I told her, "and I have nothing for breakfast. We can go out—"

"Coffee will be enough," she said, accepting a cup from me. "I have to get home, get dressed and go into the office."

"Listen," I said, as we stood there drinking coffee, "thanks for bringin' me the info about the sniper rifle."

"I don't have to tell you how much trouble I'll be in if Hicks finds out I told you," she said.

"Of if he finds out about . . . this?" I asked, indicating our present state of undress.

"This is none of his business," she said. "What I do on my own time, and who I do it with, is up to me."

"As long as you don't do it with a cop."

"No cops is my choice," she said, "but yes, you're right. As long as I want him to be my rabbi, no cops. So it wasn't a very hard choice to make."

"I hope you get what you want out of that partnership," I said.

"And I hope I didn't spoil anything between you and your neighbor."

"Don't worry about that."

"I better get dressed and get going." She put the coffee cup down on the counter. "Nick, listen, about this . . ."

"I know," I said. "It may never happen again."

"Then again," she said, "it may. Is that okay with you?"

"I'm fine with booty calls, Lydia," I said.

"Well," she said, "I really wasn't thinking of it as a booty call—"

"Yeah, you were."

"Yes," she said ruefully, "you're right, I was."

She kissed me quickly, then went and got her clothes from the sofa and went to the bedroom to put them on.

When she came out of the bedroom she looked perfect, make-up in place, ponytail back.

"How do I look?" she asked.

"Unruffled."

"I just have to look decent enough to get back home," she said.

We'd both driven our cars back from Last Exit, so there was no need for me to give her a lift.

"Is there a back way?" she asked.

"There's another door, through the office, but you don't have to do that—"

"Hey," she said, "if I come out of the office door it might look better for both of us."

I shrugged and said, "Okay."

I walked her into the office, then let her out that door. As she stepped into the hallway she looked both ways and said to me, "Empty."

She gave me another quick kiss, then wiped lipstick from my mouth with her thumb.

"Call me," she said, "if you come up with anything."

"Yeah," I said "you, too."

"Wait." She took out her card, wrote on the back, and handed it to me. "My home number's on the back. You don't necessarily have to call me at the precinct."

"What about Hicks?" I asked. "Is he gonna want to talk to me again?"

"He's pretty pissed about not getting anything from the Don," she said. "He's not convinced that The Barracuda didn't tell you something."

"He didn't," I said. "I was tellin' the truth. But I'm gonna go and talk to him again. Maybe I can get somethin' out of him with this news that you gave me."

"Okay," she said. "Let me know. And you might run into me and Hicks at the hospital."

"I'll be properly respectful, Detective Del Costa."

She smiled, said, "Bite me," and walked down the hall.

Fifty-One

I MANAGED TO GET DRESSED AND OUT WITHOUT RUNNING INTO SAM. THAT was a situation I didn't want to handle until I had to. I was going to have to decide whether or not to lie to her.

I drove directly to Victory Memorial Hospital. I wanted to see if the information Del Costa had given me would shake the Don up at all. Or maybe he could just explain it to me.

As I got out of the elevator and approached the door I saw Jacoby in front of the room, but not Po.

"Where's Hank?"

"He went to get breakfast for us and Benny."

"Burger King?"

"For Benny," Jacoby said. "Bagels or somethin' for us. How you doin'?"

"Okay," I said.

"You look . . . agitated."

"I learned somethin' new last night."

I told him about the sniper rifle round being found in my father.

"Shit, that sort of changes things," he said.

"Doesn't make sense to me that my father was the target, and then Carlo would be killed."

"So somebody tryin' to pin this on the Russians, and hit your dad by mistake?"

"I don't know," I said. "I wanna see how the Don reacts to this news. He knows somethin', I'm sure of it."

"Those detectives were pretty steamed when they didn't get anything out of him," Jacoby said. "Well, that guy, Hicks. He was pissed. The woman . . . she was hot when she got here."

"Yeah, I know," I said.

"I mean, she gave us the cold shoulder, but—"

"I know," I said, again, cutting him off. "I'm gonna go in and see what I can get from the old man."

"Good luck. I'll send Benny's breakfast in when Hank gets back."

"You guys are gonna need to clean up and get some clothes."

"We've been takin' whore's baths in the sink in the Don's bathroom," Jack said. "When the nurse's aren't lookin', you know? And we both have some fresh underwear. We're okay."

"Okay," I said. "See you when I come out."

I went inside as Benny was coming out of the bathroom.

"Just freshenin' up," he said. I could smell the excess of cologne he'd used.

"How's he doin'?" I asked.

"In and out, but when he's awake he's pretty alert. And he wants to go home."

"He's got too many holes in him for that," I said.

"I keep tellin' him that. Hey, Nick, he's real upset about your dad."

"If that's true then maybe he should help me find out who did this."

I saw Benny's ears get red.

"You still think he's lyin'?"

"About somethin', Benny," I said. "Maybe he's lyin' because he's tryin' to keep us safe, huh?"

That seemed to mollify him a bit. "You think so?"

"He thinks a lot of you," I said. "He wouldn't want you to go out and get yourself killed tryin' to avenge him."

"No, no," Benny said, "you neither, Nick."

"So I'm gonna ask him some questions, Benny," I said, "and it may sound like I'm bein' harsh, you know? But I'm really just tryin' to get to the truth. You okay with that?"

"Yeah, yeah, Nicky, I'm okay with that."

"Okay." I slapped him on the arm. "Let's do this."

Fifty-Two

WE APPROACHED THE BED AND THE OLD MAN OPENED HIS EYES. I COULD see how alert he was.

"Can you get me out of here, Nick?" he asked.

"Sure," I said. "As soon as the doctors say you can leave without dying."

He made a rude sound with his mouth and said, "Doctors. They been tellin' me for years I'm gonna die. I'm still here."

"You're still here, Uncle," I said, "but my dad isn't."

"Do not remind me," he said, putting one hand over his eyes. I saw tears roll down his face. "Vito, my old friend."

"Uncle," I said, "my dad was shot with a different weapon."

"What?"

"You were both strafed with Uzis," I explained to him. "The cops aren't sure how many. But Pop was shot with a Russian sniper rifle. One bullet through the heart. Had to be fired by a pro."

"Russians?" he said, frowning.

"Not Russians," I said. "A Russian weapon."

"You mean," Benny asked, "somebody's tryin' to make it look like it was Russians?"

I looked at him. "Maybe." I looked back at the Don. "You have to tell me what you're holdin' back, Uncle. I need the whole story."

"I am holding nothing back."

"Who would want to kill Pop?"

"They were after me," he said, slowly, "not your father."

"Then why don't you have a bullet from a Russian sniper rifle in your heart?"

He didn't answer.

"You either know who did this," I said, "or you thought you knew, and now you're not so sure. So which is it?"

He gave that some thought.

"If you're tryin' to protect me, or Benny, or anybody else, forget it," I told him. "They already killed Carlo. If they're goin' after everyone close to you, that puts us on a hit list and there's nothin' you can do about it." I leaned in closer to him. "Except help us catch 'em before they kill us all."

Now he covered his face with both hands. There were tubes sticking in both arms.

"Let's start with the phone call," I suggested. "Who was it?"

For a moment I thought he wasn't going to answer, but then he dropped his hands away from his face.

"A voice," the Don said.

"Whose voice?"

"I don't know."

"What did it say?"

"One word."

Benny and I waited.

"*Vendetta*." He said it in Italian.

"And then?"

"And then they hung up."

"Vendetta?"

"Blood feud," Benny said.

"I know what a Vendetta is," I said. "Who was it, Uncle?"

"They did not say."

"Who could it be?" I asked. "Vendetta is usually involved family against family, isn't it? What family would call Vendetta against you? And why now?"

"It could be many families from over the years," he said. "To choose one would be like . . ."

". . . a needle in a haystack?" I asked.

"*Si*."

"That can't be," I said. "This must go back many years. You are— well, you're . . ."

"Old," he said.

"Well, yeah. So someone with a Vendetta against you would also be . . . old."

"Vendetta is handed down from generation to generation," he said.

"So it could be someone's children?" I asked. "Or grandchildren?"

"Yes."

"And you?" I said. "Who is left in your family, Uncle? I mean, not Carlo, or Benny, or Pop, but an actual blood relative."

He stared up at me from the bed.

"There is only one."

I was afraid to ask.

"Who?"

"You," he said, *"figlio mio."*

My son.

Fifty-Three

I STARED AT DOMINICK BARRACONDI, THEN LOOKED AT BENNY, WHO WAS in turn staring at me with a dumfounded look on his face.

"Nick . . ." the Don said, reaching a hand out to me. "Forgive me."

"Not now," I said, backing away from the bed. "This is too much. On top of everythin' else, this is too much."

"Nick—" he called from the bed.

"Hey, Nicky—" Benny said.

But I wasn't listening to either of them. I was heading for the door. I had to get out of that room.

I burst out into the hall, surprising both Jacoby and Po.

"Nick—" Jacoby said.

"What the hell—" Hank Po said.

"I need a few minutes, guys," I said, holding my hands out to them. "I need to clear my head. That old bastard just told me I'm his son!"

I headed off down the ball, leaving them both stunned. But maybe not as stunned as me.

I found the cafeteria, got myself a bad cup of coffee and sat down at a table.

Okay, it made sense.

If Vito Delvecchio wasn't my father, who else was around back then that my mother might have been with? When we were kids Uncle Dom was always around. Who else would my mother go to if she had a problem?

We knew my parents had some problems in their marriage from time to time. Their relationship was . . . tempestuous. But the death of my older brother seemed to fix that. After he died they got closer. But by then the damage had been done. I had already been born. According to the doctor I wasn't Vito's son, and according to Dominick Barracondi, I was his.

I guess if I needed a second opinion, I'd gotten it from the horse's mouth.

I felt the floor vibrating and when I looked up saw Benny stalking towards me with a determined look on his face.

"Nicky—" he said.

"Take it easy, Benny."

"The Don just told you you're his son," Benny said. "You can't just walk out on him."

"How would you like it if you found out your dead father wasn't your father," I asked. "And then you find out that the Don is."

"If the Don told me I was his son, I'd be proud," Benny said.

"Benny, this means the Don bedded my mother."

Benny looked as if I'd slapped him. He'd never really talked about his mother, not even when we were in high school. But that had stopped him.

"Sit down, Ben," I said.

He sat.

"I'm dealin' with a lot here, man," I said. "I just need time to make some sense of it."

"Okay," Benny said, "I guess I understand that."

"If this is a Vendetta against the Don, that still doesn't explain why a sniper put a bullet in my dad's heart."

Benny remained silent.

"And if this is a Vendetta against the Don and I'm his only blood relative, then I've got a huge target on my back."

"I guess—"

"Then why was Carlo killed that night, and not me?" I asked. "You see? There's so much about this that doesn't make sense."

"Uh-oh," Benny said, looking past me.

"What?"

"More trouble."

I turned and saw Detective Sergeant Hicks heading toward me.

Benny stood up.

Fifty-Four

"BEAT IT, GUIDO," HICKS SAID, POINTING AT BENNY. "I'M HERE TO TALK TO Delvecchio."

Benny's ears reddened.

"It's okay, Benny," I said. "Go back to the Don's room."

Benny gave Hicks a hard look, then turned and stalked away.

"Is that coffee any good?" he asked, indicating the cup on the table in front of me.

"No," I said. "It's terrible."

"It's gotta be better than the crap at the office," he said. "I'll be right back."

"Where's your partner?" I asked.

"She was late this mornin'," Hicks said. "But she should be along soon. I left a message tellin' her to meet me here. You're right. I'll get her one, too."

Well, it looked like I wasn't going to get any time to myself to process my new information. It was just as well. If I'd had any spare time at all over the past couple of days I probably would have curled up into a little ball.

"Okay," Hicks said, appearing across from me. He put down a pastry and two cups of coffee, one black and one with milk, then proceeded to dump a few pounds of sugar into the milky coffee from the holder on the table.

"You ever heard of diabetes?" I asked.

"Yeah, my whole family has it," he said. "If I'm gonna get it, I'm gonna enjoy sugar while I can. Pastry? I'm not sure what kind it is, but—"

"No, not for me," I said. "What's on your mind, Sergeant?"

"Probably the same thing that's on yours," he said. "That is, if you've been tellin' the truth."

"About what?"

"About what Nicky Barracuda told you."

"He hasn't told me anything."

"And that's what he's told us," Hicks said. He bit into his pastry, licked icing from his upper lip, then sipped his coffee. "Nothin'. Only I think he knows more than he's tellin'."

"You know," I said, "that's what I think."

"Good," he said. "Then you can help us."

"How?"

"Get him to tell you what he knows, and then you tell us."

I sat back in my chair and looked at him.

"Do you have any new information?" I asked. "About my father, for instance?"

"Your father? No, nothin' new. Why?"

"I was just wonderin'."

"Look, it's the old Don who was the target, not your father," he said. "That's what we have to concentrate on. Oh, there she is."

I turned in my seat and saw Detective Del Costa coming towards us. Suit, red lipstick, hair down, very businesslike.

"Good morning," she said.

"Mornin'," we both said.

"I got you a coffee," Hicks said.

"Thanks."

"There was a pastry, but I ate it."

"That's okay."

She sat with us, removed her purse from her shoulder and hung it on the back of the chair.

"What've we got?" she asked Hicks.

"Nothin'" he said, "which is what I was tellin' Mr. Delvecchio here. We've got nothin', and he's got nothin', so maybe he can help us get somethin'."

She looked at me as if she had never seen me before.

"Oh, yes?" she said. "Going to be helpful?"

I shrugged. "If he tells me anythin', I'll let you know."

"We're gonna go talk to him while we're here," Hicks said. "You still got those two friends of yours on the door?"

"Yep."

"We've got men watching the place, you know."

"I can't see them."

"That's the point," Hicks said.

"So you're staking the Don out?"

"The Don," Hicks repeated. "You say that with such respect. He's a fuckin' gangster, for Chrissake!"

"Doesn't mean you can stake him out like a goat," I said.

"Don't worry," he said. "We'd get them before they got him."

"Or after," I said. "Wouldn't make much difference to you, would it?"

"Look—" Hicks started.

"Mr. Delvecchio," Del Costa said, "why don't you go and talk to the Don, tell him that we'll be in to see him and that he should cooperate."

"And you think he'll listen to me?"

"He'll listen to you more than he will to us," Del Costa said. I had the feeling she was trying to tell me something with her eyes.

"Okay," I said. "I'll go and talk to him, while you two finish your coffee."

"Thank you," she said.

I stood up and headed back to the Don's room.

Fifty-Five

"THE DETECTIVES ARE RIGHT BEHIND ME," I SAID TO JACOBY AND PO.

"Tough," Jacoby said. "No more bagels left."

I laughed and went inside.

"Nick?" the Don said.

I went to his bedside.

"You came back—"

"No time to talk . . . Uncle. The detectives are on their way to question you again."

"I will tell them nothing," the old man said.

"That's up to you if you want to be stubborn," I said. "Just don't tell them what you told me about . . . us."

A hurt look came into his eyes. "You are . . . ashamed."

"I don't know what I am," I said, "but I need time to figure it out. So let's just keep that little piece of information between the three of us, okay?"

He nodded and said, "As you wish."

I looked at Benny and he said, "Okay."

"I gotta go," I said. "I'll see you both later."

As I left the room I saw Hicks and Del Costa coming up the hall towards us.

"Man, she is hot," Jacoby said.

"Uh-huh," Po agreed.

I kept quiet.

As Hicks reached us he ignored Jacoby and Po and gave me a knowing look. Behind his back Del Costa gave me a whole different kind of look.

"Jesus," Po said.

"What?" Jacoby asked.

"He hit that," Po said. He looked at me. "You hit that, didn't you?"

"I'll never tell."

"He did!" Jacoby said.

"I gotta go," I said.

"What'd he tell you, Nick?" Jacoby asked. "I mean, about . . . you know."

"Nothin' yet," I said. "I haven't had a chance to talk to him about it. Hell, I haven't even had a minute alone to think about it."

"Maybe that's for the best," Po said.

"Yeah," I said, "I'll deal with it all after this is over."

"Is he gonna tell them anythin'?" Po asked, jerking his head toward the door.

"I doubt it."

"Then you better get out of here before they come lookin' for you."

"Good advice," I said, stating down the hall. "I'll be in touch."

I got out of the hospital. Now where to? I was armed with new information—the Russian sniper rifle, and the little fact that the Don was claiming to be my father. I decided to drive over to Pop's house and see if Maria and Father Vinnie were still there. I wanted to talk to Vinnie but wondered if I was going to be able to do it without Maria around?

I parked out front and hoped there wouldn't be such a crowd in the house today. I know they liked my dad, but couldn't they wait for his wake?

As I entered I realized I hadn't asked either Hicks or Del Costa when we could have the body for a funeral. I knew their case was still ongoing, but if Hicks was so sure that the shooters were after the Don, why not release Vito's body?

Vito! When had I ever thought of my dad as Vito? Already I was starting to think of him differently.

I entered the house with my key. "Hello?" I called. "Anybody home?"

"In the kitchen!" Maria shouted.

I joined her there. She had containers and bowls out and seemed to be consolidating food to make more room in the refrigerator.

"Hey, where's Vinnie?"

"He had to go to work," she said.

"They're pushing him to come back?"

"No, no," she said, "they'll give him as much time as he wants, but one of the priests got sick, so he's covering. Why?" She looked up from the Tupperware she was closing. "Is there something you can talk to him about and not me?"

"What? No. What makes you think that?"

"Because now that you know he's not here you're edging towards the door."

Suddenly, my stomach was growling and I remembered all I'd had so far was my own bad coffee and the hospital's worse.

"I tell you what," I said. "You make me somethin' to eat and I'll tell you what I was gonna tell Vinnie."

Fifty-Six

"HE SAID *WHAT?*"

We decided to keep Mrs. Delgado's lasagna for dinner, so Maria heated up somebody's tuna casserole for me.

"He told me he's my father."

"You mean Uncle Dom and Mom . . ."

"That's what it means."

She took a moment to try to digest what I'd told her, then asked, "Do you believe him?"

I dropped my fork, letting it clink into my plate and put my elbows on the table.

"I don't know what to believe, Maria," I said. "I've got things comin' at me from all sides."

And I included in that Detective Del Costa's booty call—as if I didn't have enough to think about.

"But Ma, cheatin' on Pop?" she asked.

"We know they had some trouble," I said. "They never made a secret of that."

"Yeah, but they got over it."

"Well, maybe she was with Uncle Dom during that time."

She hesitated, then asked, "So, does this mean you're in the Mafia?"

"Yeah, probably," I said. "I'll probably have to kill somebody so I can be a made man."

"Nick!"

"Of course I'm not in the Mafia, Maria." I picked my fork up again.

"I was just asking."

I decided not to tell Maria about the "Vendetta" talk. For one thing, why push everything that was burdening me onto her shoulders? For another, it sounded so fucking dramatic.

"What are you going to do when you finish eatin'?" she asked.

I shrugged. "I guess I'll go and see Vinnie," I said.

And tell him the rest that I didn't tell her, like the stuff about the Russian sniper rifle.

"Nick, do you want me to go to the hospital and give Benny some time to go home and change?"

"You could try," I said. "I don't think Benny's gonna leave the Don's side for a second."

"Maybe I should go and just give him someone to talk to, huh?"

"That sounds good," I said. It would also get her out of the house. Vito's house. My father's—*her* father's house.

Ah, shit.

Vinnie worked at the Church of the Holy Family, in Canarsie. The church was on the corner of Flatlands Avenue and Rockaway Parkway, the school at the other end of the block. The Rectory was positioned between them.

At one time this was considered one of the well-to-do parishes in Brooklyn, but things had begun to change. The original owners of many of the homes in the area had started to sell and move away. How to put this without sounding like a bigot? Less desirable types had begun to move in.

I stopped at the front door of the Rectory and rang the bell. A priest I didn't know, white-haired and slightly bent, answered.

"I'm here to see Father Vincent."

"Do you have an appointment?"

"I'm his brother, Nick." Unless I suddenly found out that we didn't even have the same mother!

"Oh, of course," he said. "Come in. I'll tell him you're here."

I waited just inside the door. There wasn't a sound in the place. As a kid the Rectory had always felt more eerie to me than even the big churches had.

Vinnie came down the hall and said, "Hey, Nick, come on up."

He took me up to his room on the second floor. It was not large and was very simply furnished. The only sign that it was my brother's was a bookshelf full of paperbacks. Agatha Christie, Andrew Greeley, and G.K. Chesterton's Father Brown, among others.

"I had to come in and cover for Father Paul—" he started to explain, but I cut him off.

"Maria told me."

"Why are you here?"

"Well, you guys both told me you wanted me to check in."

"And you said you couldn't be checking in with us all the time, so somethin's wrong. What is it?"

"More . . . weird news."

"Like what?"

He sat quietly while I told him about the Russian sniper, what the implications of that could be, and then hit him with the *"figlio mio"* stuff last.

Fifty-Seven

VINNIE SAT THERE, STUNNED.

"I don't know what shocks me the most," he said, "that the Don is your father, or that Pop might've been the target."

"Yeah, well . . . it's all been kind of shockin', hasn't it?"

"Nicky . . ." He reached out and put a hand on my knee. He was sitting on the edge of his bed, and I was in the room's only chair.

"I know, I know," I said, "you're still my brother, Maria's still my sister."

"And the Russians killed Pop?"

"I think the Uzis are supposed to make us suspect the Jamaicans, and the rifle is supposed to make us suspect the Russians."

"Then who did it?"

"Well," I said, slowly, "I haven't told you about the Vendetta."

Just the word "Vendetta" conjures up a gray-haired old Italian woman flicking her thumb off her gold front teeth.

"What?" Vinnie said.

I told him how I knew the Don was holding something back and was finally able to drag it out of him.

"Was he serious, Nick?"

"Looked pretty serious to me."

"So is he gonna tell the cops?"

"I don't know what he's gonna tell them, but I asked him not to tell them that I'm his son. When I told Maria she asked me if that meant I was in the Mafia. What are the cops gonna think?"

"They'll never believe you didn't know, will they?"

"No," I said, "suddenly, I'll be Michael Corleone in their eyes."

"Nick," Vinnie said, "maybe you should just back off and let the police handle it. All of it."

"I could do that, Vin," I said, "but if the Don is right, if I'm his son and this is a Vendetta, then I won't be allowed to do that. They'll come after me."

I'd tried to figure this out six ways from Sunday, talked it out with a few people. What I hadn't done was sit in a room by myself and give it all some good, hard, analytical thought.

Like Father Vinnie said.

All of it.

Vinnie walked me down to the door with his arm around my shoulder.

"What a mess," he said.

"Yeah," I said, "a confusing mess."

"I don't know how you can concentrate. I guess it's that detective's brain of yours. What Hercule Poirot calls 'the little gray cells.'"

"I think I need a drink," I said. "Or lots of drinks. What does Poirot say about that?"

"I think he's a teetotaler."

"Yeah, well, tea ain't gonna do it," I said. "I'm sure even Father Brown went into the sacrificial wine, sometimes."

He slapped me on the back as I opened the door. He said, "Let me know what happens—and when we can get Pop's body and plan the funeral."

"Okay, Vin," I said. "I'll be in touch."

Fifty-Eight

I DROVE BACK TO MY PLACE. THIS TIME I WAS HOPING MY MESSAGE machine would be flashing, and that it would be Winky with some information. But if there wasn't a hit out on the Don, what could Winky even find out for me?

For a change the red light was off. I slammed my door, then realized this would probably attract Sam's attention. I still had to explain to her why I wasn't around for breakfast.

I waited, listening for her door to open, and when it didn't I assumed I lucked out and she wasn't home.

I took off my windbreaker, still weighed down by the gun in my pocket. I was sure Hicks had noticed, but he hadn't said a word. I might not be so lucky next time, but I did have a permit so it would just be a matter of whether or not he wanted to give me a hard time. The cops could always pull my license and confiscate my gun while they examined my qualifications. It had been tried before, but I had hardly any shooting incidents on my record.

I went into the bathroom to wash up, found the terry cloth robe Del Costa had worn hanging on the door, still smelling like her. I knew my sheets would smell of her, too, so I'd have to change them or try to sleep with blue balls all night.

Not that I'd been getting much sleep.

Suddenly, as I was drying my hands, sleep seemed like a damned good idea. I didn't even bother with the sheets. I shucked my clothes, wrapped myself in the Del Costa sheets, and was asleep in moments, despite the daylight.

It was dark when I woke up. I was confused. I didn't know what time of day it was. I looked at my window and saw that the shade was up. After a few moments my eyes got used to the darkness and I realized it wasn't *that* late.

I turned onto my back and then stopped. Something had woke me up. What was it? I'd had a thought, but now I couldn't retrieve it. I listened, and then I heard it.

Somebody was in the office.

Sam?

Or somebody with Vendetta on their mind?

Jeez, where was my gun? Oh yeah, in my jacket pocket. Where was my jacket?

I got off the bed.

To get to the office I had to walk through the entire apartment. It was dark, but not pitch black. I was wearing only my boxers, and no shoes. I managed not to stub my toe anywhere.

Behind my front door I always kept a Mickey Mantle baseball bat for emergencies. I got my hands on it, and then crept toward the office, holding it ready.

And at that moment there was a knock at the door.

I stopped. Not a sound came from the office. Then I heard the office door opening. I'd been meaning to oil those hinges.

I turned and ran for my front door. To get off the floor the intruder had to go by there. I heard noise in the hall, the sound of somebody hitting the floor. I swung the door open with the bat ready.

Sam looked up at me from the floor, and pointed down the hall.

"He went that way!"

"You all right?"

"Go!"

I ran down the hall, into the stairwell. I could hear him pounding down the stairs, but it wasn't easy to chase somebody when I was only wearing boxer shorts and no shoes.

I made it as far as the main floor, but he was out the door and gone. I stopped at the front door, looking both ways, saw somebody hotfooting it down the street.

I put the bat on my shoulder and walked back upstairs. Sam was still in the hallway, leaning against the wall and rubbing her left foot.

"You okay?" I asked.

"He stomped on my foot," she said.

"Come on." I grabbed her arm and helped her into my place.

I put her on the sofa and said, "Let me get dressed."

"Go ahead."

I was in the bedroom pulling on my pants when she yelled, "So you were in the bedroom and he was creepin' around your office?"

"Yeah," I called out. "Believe it or not, I finally fell asleep."

"So what was he lookin' for?"

"I don't know." I stepped back into the room, dressed. "Why don't we find out? Can you walk?"

"Yeah."

She got up and we walked to the office. I turned on the light.

"So it was a he?"

"Definitely a he," she said. "Tall guy, but not husky."

"Fast, too," I said. "I saw him running down the street. Even if I'd been dressed I don't think I could've caught him."

I went to my desk, stood behind it, and surveyed the room for anything out of place.

"And if he had a gun, what were you gonna do with your bat?"

"Hit a home run, hopefully," I said, still scanning the room.

"Anything missing?" she asked.

"Nothing missing," I said, "nothing disturbed."

"You can tell?"

She looked around. Maybe it was a little messy, but I knew where things went.

"I can tell."

"So then who was it? A burglar? Or a killer, lying in wait?"

"'Lying in wait?'" I asked. "Have you ever really written that line?"

"Just last night, actually," she said. "Beer?"

"Let's go."

We left the office and went to the kitchen. She went into the fridge, came out with two Rolling Rocks. "So how did it go with your lady detective?" she asked.

I froze.

Fifty-Nine

"COME ON, NICK," SHE SAID. "THE GOOD STUFF'S GONE. YOUR NEWCASTLE? You only pull those out for special situations. I knocked this morning, you didn't answer, but I knew you were home. And then she came walking out of your office. What'd she do, show up on your doorstep at dawn?"

I studied her, to see if she was playing games. She wasn't, but I thought she was giving me an out. After all, who has Newcastle for breakfast?

"No," I said, "she spent the night."

She sipped her beer.

"She wanted to meet the night before, so I picked Last Exit, only it was too crowded to talk."

"Could've went down the street to Pete's."

"She didn't want to go anywhere we might be seen by other cops."

"Don't tell me, let me guess," Sam said. "She doesn't do cops."

"No, she doesn't."

"So you ended up here?"

"Right."

"And you couldn't answer the doctor and tell me to go away?"

"Uh, no."

She sipped her beer again.

"So what'd you find out?"

"The killing shot on my dad didn't come from an Uzi, it came from a Russian Dragunov."

"A Russian sniper rifle?"

I stared at her.

"What? I do my research."

"I'm impressed."

"So what's it all mean?"

"A heart shot, just like the driver, Carlo."

"That doesn't make sense," she said. "I could see Carlo and the Don, but this . . ."

"I know," I said. "I've hashed and rehashed it."

"There's something else, isn't there?"

"Yeah," I said. "The Don says it's some kind of Vendetta."

"For real?"

"Yeah, for real."

"So anyone close to him or related to him, is in danger?"

"Blood relatives."

"Does he have any?"

"Just one."

She stared at me, then put her hand over her mouth and took a deep breath.

"Oh, Nick."

"Yeah."

"Do the cops know?"

"No," I said. "Not from me, anyway. They went in to talk to the old man today."

"Do you think he told them?"

"We agreed he wouldn't, but who knows?"

"How sharp is he?"

"Very sharp."

"Then he won't blurt it out by accident?"

"No."

"So this, tonight, a killer?"

"Probably."

"Nick, you need to be careful."

"Yeah," I said, "better locks."

"More than that," she said. "You need to hide."

"Hide?" I asked. "That's one alternative I didn't think of."

"No, you wouldn't. Let me ask you this. If you're included in this

Vendetta because you're a blood relation to Dominick Barracondi, are Maria and Father Vinnie at risk because they're your blood relatives?"

I stared at her over my green bottle and then said, "Oh, shit."

Sixty

"YOU WANT ME TO WHAT?" FATHER VINNIE ASKED.

I was sitting on my sofa watching Sam drink beer from a bottle—always a pleasure—talking to Vinnie, who I called on the phone at the Rectory.

"Take Maria and go on a vacation," I said. "Maybe Florida."

Sam shook her head violently.

"What?" I asked.

"Everybody goes there. Tell him to go someplace else."

"There's a monastery," Vinnie said, "a retreat. We could—"

"No," I said. "Vin, that's too obvious."

"Not for Maria."

"She's Catholic, isn't she?"

"Well, yeah . . ."

"Well, yeah . . . and what do you mean, not for her?" I asked.

"Well, I assume you're worried about us."

"Good guess."

"So I agree that Maria should go away."

"But not you."

"I'm needed here, Nick."

"Vinnie—"

"Father Vincent."

"Don't pull rank with me."

"Maine," Sam said. "That's where I'd go."

"Great," I said. "Nobody in my family would ever think of that."

"Of what?" Vinnie asked.

"Maine."

"What about Maine?"

"Go . . . to . . . Maine!" I shouted into the phone.

"Nick," he said, "what happened tonight?"

I told him.

"What the hell—sorry—heck were you gonna do with a baseball bat against a gun?" he asked.

"You're not the first person to ask me that," I said, "and it was a Mickey Mantle."

"And because somebody broke into your office you want me and Maria to go into hiding?"

"Look, Vinnie, it's this Vendetta thing."

"What about it?"

I laid it out for him the way Sam had laid it out for me.

He was quiet. Then he said, "You just worked that out tonight?"

"Um, well, Sam asked me the question."

"Well . . . it's a good one," he said. "But maybe before we go into hiding you should ask someone if that's really what happened to him."

"Like who?"

"Like the Don."

That was probably a good idea.

"So you're gonna go to the hospital and talk it all over with . . . the Don?" Sam asked.

"If I get this part cleared up, I can stop thinking about it. Then maybe I can solve the shooting."

"So you're gonna go tonight?"

I checked my watch.

"Visiting hours are over," I said, "but the two men on the door *are* workin' for me."

"Nick?" she said. "Let's get something to eat, then you can go back to bed, get some more rest and go see the Don in the morning."

"I should do it tonight . . ."

I realized I was hungry.

"You think this guy's going right from here to Father Vinnie's? Or Maria's?"

"Maria," I said. "I should go and see Maria." I looked at her. "Did you go see her?"

"I was going to," she said, squirming, "but I got involved in my book, and—"

"It doesn't matter," I said. "Come with me now."

"Nick, I have to—"

"Wait."

I called my father's house. The phone rang five times and I was just starting to get worried when Maria answered.

"Where were you?"

"I went to the hospital to see Benny," she said. "I just got back."

"Okay, stay there. I'm comin' over and I'm bringin' company."

"To eat?"

"Yes."

"Good," she said. "I'll pull out the lasagna."

I hung up and looked at Sam.

"There's food," I said. "Lots of it. The whole neighborhood turned out."

"You're inviting me to dinner with you and your family?" she asked.

"Yes."

I dialed the Rectory, got Vinnie again.

"Now what?"

"Food, at Pop's, tonight," I said.

"Yeah, sure," he said. "I'm hungry. Is there still some of Mrs. Delgado's lasagna?"

"We haven't touched it yet."

"See you there."

We hung up.

"Ready?" I asked Sam.

"Sure, why not?"

Sixty-One

WE WENT DOWNSTAIRS AND GOT IN MY CAR.

"What were you comin' to see me about tonight?" I asked.

"You mean when I interrupted your plan to go up against a killer with a Louisville Slugger?"

"A Special Mickey Mantle Louisville Slugger."

"Okay!"

"You know who Mickey Mantle was, right?"

"Yes," she said, "I've been in New York that long. And I was just coming to see if you wanted to eat. I was going to heat something up, but I like this better." We drove in silence for a while and then she said, "You're too honest sometimes, you know."

"Am I? Oh, you mean tellin' Vinnie that it was your idea that he and Maria—"

"No," she said, "I didn't mean that. I gave you every out with your lady detective."

"Oh, that," I said.

"Yes, that."

"We're friends, Sam," I said. "Close friends. I didn't want to lie to you."

"Nick . . . what you do in your own apartment is your business."

"Yeah, I know . . ."

"But?"

"I didn't plan it," I said.

"I know," she said, staring straight ahead. "It just happened."

"It just happened," I repeated, and then there it was. The thought I'd woken up with, and lost.

I turned the car around.

"What are you doing?"

"One stop," I said.

When Catherine opened the door she looked at Sam, and then me, and asked, "Was there something else you wanted to talk to me about, Nick?"

"The last time we talked you said Mary Ann slept well, that she didn't take sleeping pills."

"That's right."

"Is your mother home? I'd like to talk to her."

"Come on in," she said. "She's in Mary Ann's room."

I looked at Sam.

I'll wait here," she said.

"I went down the hall and found Mary Ann's mother sitting alone the way I had left her when I saw her last.

"Angela?"

For a moment it seemed as if she hadn't heard me, then she suddenly looked up.

"Nick?" she said. "What are you doing here? You have your own family to think of—"

"It's okay," I said. "I just have some things to ask you."

"Oh, well, all right. Come, sit."

I moved into the room, sat at the foot of the bed, leaving some space between us.

"Tell me about Mary Ann, Angela."

"What about her?"

"What kind of child was she?"

She got a faraway look in her eyes. "She was a beautiful child, so beautiful. Obedient, when she was younger . . ."

"And when did she change?"

"Change?"

"You know what I mean. Was it in high school? When she got boy crazy?"

"Boy crazy? What do you mean?"

"I've read her poetry, Angela. I've talked with Catherine . . . and with Sal."

"Sal . . ."

"You know Sal, Angela. You know a lot of things."

She remained silent.

I moved closer to her. "Come on, Angela. Tell me about Mary Ann. Tell me what she was really like."

She waited a long time to answer me, and I waited with her. I didn't want to hear any more of that "beautiful child" stuff and if the truth was going to come out, I was willing to wait.

Finally she looked at me and her expression was totally different. No longer was she the mother in mourning. Now she was the dissatisfied mother, the long-suffering mother.

"She was disrespectful," she said. "She was . . . bad . . . a trial, Nick, believe me. She was . . . wild. Everyone thought she was such a saint, but—"

"Who's everyone, Angela?"

"My friends, our relatives," she said. "Tony. She had him totally fooled. She had them all fooled. That don't know what she was like when she discovered boys and . . . sex!" She said the word as if it had four letters, not three. "She had sex for the first time in junior high school. Did you know that?"

I didn't know that, but what could I say?

"She was . . . uncontrollable! But she was smart."

"Smart enough to fool everybody but you, huh, Angela?" I asked. "And Sal. She couldn't fool Sal."

"Sal," she said, shaking her head. "What she did to that poor boy."

"You mean . . . the rape?"

"Rape!" she spat. "There was no rape. I think Sal may have been the only boy to give her exactly what she wanted."

"Why was she marrying Tony, then?"

"Why? Because she said she had changed, that's why. Saw the *light*. That after she had spent her life doing things no Catholic girl should ever do."

She averted her eyes. She didn't look at me, or out the window, but at the crucifix that was on the wall.

"She said God forgave her, and she wanted me to forgive her."

"But you couldn't?"

"I knew she hadn't changed. I knew she'd go back to making my life miserable, and she'd do it to Tony."

"So you killed her."

"I did not!" she said, her head snapping toward me, her eyes flashing. "She was my daughter, for God's sake."

"Angela, the police found a bottle of sleeping pills in her room. They were yours."

"She must have . . . taken them."

"But they were in your bathroom, Angela. Your daughters never went into your bathroom. Never."

"She was bad," Angela said. "She'd do . . . anything."

"But why go upstairs to get the pills and then downstairs to take them? And why leave the container on the sink?"

"I . . . I don't know. She must have taken them."

"Did she, Angela?" I asked. "Did she do that? O did you give them to her?"

"I did not *force* her to take them."

"Maybe you didn't force her," I said, "but you gave them to her, didn't you?"

She looked at me, then away, back at the crucifix.

"I—I didn't know what to do. I prayed for guidance. If she stayed here . . . got married. . . eventually people would find out . . . what she was really like."

"What if she really had changed? How about that?" I asked. "What if she married Tony, made him a good wife, and had grandchildren?"

"She wouldn't . . ." she said, shaking her head. "She wouldn't. . . ."

"Well, you'll never know, Angela," I said, "because you badgered her into taking those pills."

"I told her, if she had really changed there was only one way to get right with God."

"Suicide?" I asked. "Suicide is a mortal sin, Angela. Not exactly the way to get right with God, is it? No, you wanted her to get right with you, and dead she could never disgrace you again."

She remained silent.

"Did you sit with her, Angela? Watch her take them? Or did you leave her alone? Let her die alone." I got in her face, so she couldn't turn away. "Did you actually tell your own daughter she'd be better off dead?"

"I did the right thing," she said. "I know I did."

I left the room. She was still saying it, over and over, trying to convince herself.

Sixty-Two

"SO WHAT ARE YOU GOING TO DO?" SAM ASKED IN THE CAR. "TELL THE police?"

"I can tell them," I said, "but I can't prove anything. Angela would have to admit it. And even if she did, she's right. She didn't *force* those pills down Mary Ann's throat."

"But . . . she was responsible."

"For what?" I asked. "She gave her pills. She didn't mean to kill her daughter. It just . . . happened."

When we got to the house Vinnie hadn't arrived yet. Sam and Maria hugged and then went to the kitchen together. I stayed in the living room, waiting for Vinnie. I was tired of hashing and rehashing things out in a half-assed fashion because I was actually trying *not* to think about who my father was. Maybe with these three people—the people I felt closest to—I could work things out and clear my head.

When Vinnie arrived I had to admit it had a calming effect on me to see him wearing his collar. On other men the white collar affected me the way a red flag affects a bull.

We embraced briefly then he went into the kitchen and came back with two Rolling Rocks.

"The girls said dinner will be ready in a few minutes," he said. "It's nice to see Sam here."

"Yeah," I said.

"What did you do?" he asked.

"What do you mean?"

"That look on your face, it's the same one you had when they caught you in a closet in fifth grade with Bernadette McDonald."

"You're crazy—"

"Come on," he said, lowering his voice, "who were you in the closet with this time?"

I took a swig from my bottle and then said, "Detective Del Costa."

"With all the black hair?" he said, eyes wide. "Jesus. I thought you said she was a ballbuster—"

"Father Vinnie!"

"I'm just quoting you."

"I don't think I ever said that."

"Well, you insinuated it."

"Maybe that's her reputation in the department, but . . ."

"Jeez, Nick," he said, "what's wrong with you? Well, I hope you had the good sense not to go to your own apartment."

I kept quiet.

"You did it right across the hall from Sam?"

"Look, Vinnie," I said, "Sam and I are friends—"

"Are you gonna be this dense all your life?"

"Vinnie," I said, bringing my voice even lower, "I didn't come here to talk about me and Sam, okay? I've got enough on my mind."

"Okay, okay . . ."

Sam and Maria came out of the kitchen carrying bowls and plates and Maria said, "It would be nice if someone went into the kitchen and brought out the drinks . . ."

". . . and the silverware," Sam said.

"On it!" I said and Vinnie and I ran and obeyed.

Over Mrs. Delgado's lasagna and Mrs. Benedetti's antipasto I tried to work everything out in front of a captive audience.

I hashed, rehashed and re-rehashed it while they ate and listened. When I was done they all stared at me.

"I got nothin'," Vinnie finally said. "I'm a priest, not a detective. I still say you've got to ask the Don about the blood thing. If we're not in danger there's no reason for us to go anywhere."

He looked at Maria, who simply shrugged and said, "I'm just a girl."

That didn't sit well with Sam. She hated women who adopted that attitude and I admired her for not smacking my sister in the back of the head.

"Okay," she said, "I know I'm the one who brought up the question of Vinnie and Maria being in danger, but now I don't think it's true."

"Why not?" I asked.

"Well," she said, "even if you are related to the Don, who knows that? Just you, him and Benny, right?"

"Right."

"So why would the Vendetta extend to them?"

We all looked at her.

"She's right," Vinnie said. "We're safe if nobody knows."

"So basically," I commented, "if you hadn't said a word about this we wouldn't have spent all this time talkin' about it."

She stared at me and asked, "Are you saying I should've just kept my mouth shut?"

"No, no," Vinnie said, "he's not saying that."

"No," I said, "that's not what I meant . . ."

"More lasagna, anyone?" Maria asked.

Sixty-Three

THE BIGGEST QUESTION WE COULD COME UP WITH WAS: IF POP WAS THE target, why?

"If the Don's right," Vinnie said, "and it's Vendetta, maybe they hit Pop because he was Dominick's closest friend."

"I'm his godson," I said. "Why kill Carlo when I was right there, out in the open? Or why not Benny? The Don is closer to Benny than he was to Carlo."

"Can I speak?" Sam asked.

"Of course you can," I said, wishing I hadn't said a word, earlier.

"Maybe they haven't been able to get a shot at Benny, especially since he's been inside the hospital all this time. And where was he when the first shooting took place?"

"Inside the restaurant."

"There you go."

"And me?" I asked.

"Maybe," she said, "they're just saving you for the end."

I called the hospital and got them to put me through to the Don's room by telling them it was a life-or-death emergency.

Benny answered. Instead of telling him everything and having him relay it to Jacoby or Po I did it the other way around. I told him to put one of them on the phone.

Jacoby came on.

"What's up, Nick?"

"I caught somebody creeping around my office tonight, Jack," I said.

"You thinking they were gonna make a try at you?"

"Maybe," I said. "He got scared away before we could find out. But nothin' was missin', so I think he was just waitin' in there for me."

"Okay, well, we'll keep on our toes. You gettin' any sleep?"

"Maybe too much. I'll talk to you later."

"Okay."

"Look, stay together, okay? You, Hank and Benny, don't let anybody catch one of you alone."

"We got it, Nick. Later."

I hung up, looked at Sam, who was standing in the kitchen doorway looking at me. Behind her Vinnie and Maria were cleaning the kitchen.

"Ready to go?" she asked.

"Yep," I said, standing up.

We hugged and kissed Vinnie and Maria, and left.

"I'm sorry," I said, as I drove.

"About what?"

"I didn't mean—"

"I know you didn't mean it," she said, "but you were right. If I hadn't brought it up you wouldn't have had to deal with it, at all."

"But you didn't know that at the time. You were tryin' to help."

"I'll always try to help you, Nick."

All my life I was either "Nicky" or "Nicky D" to people, but to Sam it was always "Nick."

"I know you will, Sam, and I appreciate it."

"So what's happening with you and the lady detective?" she asked.

"Nothing, as far as I can tell."

I explained the situation to her and she started laughing.

"What's so funny?"

"You were her booty call."

"I came to that conclusion all by myself."

"And do you feel . . . used?"

"Actually, no," I said.

She laughed again.

"Just like a man," she said, "and you're all man, Nick."

I didn't know if she meant that was good or bad.

Sixty-Four

THE RED LIGHT, BLINKING, BLINKING.

"Nick," Benny's voice said, "the Don wants to talk to you. He wants you to come and see him in the mornin'."

The second message was from Winky: "Delvecchio, I've got some information for you. I'll call you at eight a.m. and tell you where to meet me."

The third was from Lydia Del Costa: "Call me."

The red light stopped blinking.

It occurred to me that this case was probably going to have to be solved without benefit of real detective work. If Winky could tell me something, and the Don could tell me something, it would just be a matter of putting the information together. Information that the police would not have.

Unless I shared it.

If this was a Vendetta being pursued by one man I could probably handle it, but if it was being perpetrated by a group, I would need help. And if I needed help I'd go to Del Costa.

There was a time when I had a friend high up in the department, but Inspector Ed Gorman had retired several years ago. The older I got, the less valuable my time on the job became, because the men I had worked for, or with, had moved on, or had not moved up very far in the Department—or had died.

My connection to Lydia Del Costa, at the moment, was my most valuable Department asset. The only other one I might have called on was Detective Weinstock, who was also in Homicide.

I had said goodnight to Sam at her door. No promise of breakfast in the morning. No arrangement for a knock at the door.

I could have gone to bed without acting on any of the three calls. I couldn't call Winky because I didn't have a number. Could have called Benny and gotten the call put through as another emergency, but it wasn't necessary.

I certainly could have called Del Costa back, but what if it was another booty call? As Sam had said, I was all man, and probably wouldn't have been able to resist.

I decided to do nothing until the morning. I got myself ready for bed, put fresh sheets on the mattress, and turned in for the night.

The phone jarred me awake. I grabbed it before it could ring a second time. I checked the clock. It was 7:58 a.m.

"What?"

"Delvecchio?"

"Yeah."

"It's Winky, man. I got somethin' for ya."

"Hey, Winky," I said, rubbing my eyes. "Wait a minute." I held the phone against my chest while I hacked until my throat was clear. How bad would it have been if I smoked?

"Whataya got, Winky?"

"I got two Jamaicans braggin' that they took out a Mafia Don."

I sat up straight in bed.

"Where are they?" I asked. "Who are they?"

"They're a couple of would-be drug lords who take on work like this," Winky said. "But they have big mouths, so nobody's been usin' them lately."

But somebody did, I thought, maybe *because* they have big mouths. Somebody set them up for this.

"Where do I find them, Winky?"

"East Flatbush. They hang out in a bar on Utica Avenue and East Fifty-First Street. Place called Kingston's."

"A dive?"

"Definitely. Don't go near it without a gun."

"You got names for me, right, Winky?"

"One's called Huntley," Winky said, "the other one is Dalton."

"No last names?"

"Last names ain't special, Delvecchio," he said. "'cept maybe for Dagos You're lookin' for Huntley and Dalton. I don't know if they're your men, but they're sure braggin' like they are."

"Thanks, Winky."

"This worth somethin'?"

"It's worth a lot. Don't worry, you'll get paid. Especially if you come up with the name of the sniper."

"Yeah, well, I'm still workin' on that. If it was a Russian it'll be a little harder. If it was somebody tryin' ta frame the Russians, I might be able ta do somethin'."

"Okay," I said, "I'll be waiting."

I hung up, called the hospital and managed to get put through to the Don's room. Benny answered on the first ring.

"Where the hell are ya, Nicky?" he asked. "The Don wants ya."

"And I want to talk to him, too, Benny," I said, calmly, still giving him the benefit of the doubt because he was upset, "but I just got a tip on the guys with the Uzis."

"You gonna check it out?"

"Yeah, but later," I said "It's a dive called Kingston's in East Flatbush, won't be open this early."

"Then what's the hold-up?"

"The cops want to talk to me, too," I said, "so I'm probably gonna have to go see them before I come to the hospital."

"Yeah, okay, but then hurry."

"Is he okay?"

"Who know? He's still hooked up to machines and the beepin' is drivin' me crazy."

"Benny, I think the trouble starts when the beeping stops."

"Yeah, yeah, I know. See ya, Nicky."

I hung up and decided to get myself showered, dressed and coffeed before I called anyone else.

Sixty-Five

I HAD A SECOND CUP OF COFFEE BEFORE I FISHED OUT DETECTIVE DEL Costa's number and dialed it.

"You're up and around early," she said.

"The phone woke me," I said. "What's goin' on?"

"Hicks wanted me to bounce this off you," she said.

"What?"

"Your friend Benny."

"What about him?"

"We're looking at him for this."

"Wait," I said. "You're lookin' at Benny for the attempt on the Don? And the shootin' of my father?"

"Yes, what do you think?"

"No way," I said. "Benny would cut off his left arm before he hurt the Don. And he'd never do anything to hurt my dad."

"You're sure?"

"I'd bet my life on it," I said. "Benny has been loyal to the Don for twelve years, or so. He loves the Don."

"Okay," she said. "I'll tell Hicks."

"What put you on this track?"

"Hicks is running the investigation," she said, "and he doesn't always clue me in. Anyway, thanks."

"Wait, that's all you wanted?"

"Yes," she said. "Why? Was there something else?"

"Nope," I said. "Not for me."

"Okay, then," she said, and hung up.

The kind of girl every guy wants, right? Booty call the night before, attitude like nothing ever happened the next day.

Okay, sure. Why not?

When I got to the hospital Jacoby was alone at the Don's door.

"We decided to work in shifts," he told me. "Hank will relieve me in about an hour."

"Sure, fine," I said. "Whatever works. I'm hoping I won't have to keep you here much longer."

"You got a solid lead?"

"I do," I said, and told him about my 8 a.m. call.

"Want me to go with you?" Jacoby asked.

"No," I said. "I might take Benny, though."

"Why?"

"Because I might not have a choice. I don't know that I'll be able to stop him."

I went into the room. Benny was standing at the Don's bed, staring down at the old man. I moved closer just as the Don's eyes opened. They were sunken and bloodshot, his face shiny with perspiration, jaw covered by gray stubble.

"He's been askin' for you," Benny said, backing away from the bed.

I took his place, stared down at the man who claimed to be my real father.

"Nicky," he said, grabbing for my hand, "Vendetta, Vendetta . . ."

I stared into his eyes. They didn't seem to be focusing. He knew who I was, but beyond that he only seemed able to say that one word.

"Benny, what—" I started, turning, but Benny was not in the room. "Benny?"

I ran to the bathroom, but he wasn't there, either. He was gone.

I opened the door and asked Jack, "Where's Benny?"

"He just left. Said something about fixing things."

"Great."

"Where could he be going?" Jacoby asked.

"Only one place that I know of," I said. "Jack . . ."

"I know," he said. "Stay here."

"Thanks."

●

IF BENNY had gone off halfcocked he was on his way to East Flatbush to find those two Jamaicans. I had served them up to him on a platter.

I drove as fast as I could to Utica and Fifty-First. The area, right near Linden Boulevard, had a large Jamaican population. I pulled up in front of the Kingston Bar, parked illegally. I wasn't the only one. Benny's Fleetwood was half on the sidewalk.

I was heading for the door when I heard the shots—definitely an Uzi.

I rushed inside with my gun in my hand as more shots rang out, but singles. When I got inside it was over. Benny was standing there with his .45 in his hand. The two Jamaicans were down.

"Benny! What the hell?"

He turned and looked at me.

"When I walked in they went for their Uzis," he said, pointing.

Beneath the table the Jamaicans must have been seated at was a gym bag—big enough to hold the two Uzis that were on the floor. The ceiling had holes in it, stitched by an Uzi. The bartender who had been crouched behind the bar, stood up slowly.

"What hoppen, Mon?" he demanded, glancing up. "Look at me ceilin'."

"Did you call the cops?"

"Yeah, I call dem—"

"Just relax."

"Relax, Mon?" the man asked. "He kill two of me best customers." He pointed at Benny.

"You always let customers in carrying Uzis?"

"I don't know what me customers are carryin', Mon."

"Yeah, well, tell it to the cops." I could hear the sirens. "Benny, give me the gun before they get here."

"What for?" he asked. "All I did was defend myself."

"Yeah, but you came here to kill them," I said.

"No . . . I didn't, Nick . . ."

"Yeah, you did. Come on, give it to me before they come through the door." I put my gun away and held my hand out for his. The sirens pulled up out front. He handed me the gun.

Sixty-Six

"WHY DIDN'T YOU TELL ME THIS MORNING ON THE PHONE?" DETECTIVE Del Costa asked.

"I didn't know, then," I lied. "I got the call after we talked, and then I was in a hurry."

"No," she said, "that won't wash. You told me that the phone woke you up. You got the tip before we spoke."

"Okay, look," I said. "I just wanted to make sure the tip was good, then I would have called you."

"So instead, you told Benny?"

"That," I said, "was bad judgment on my part, I admit."

We were in an interview room at her headquarters. I'd convinced the patrol cops not to shoot us, and to call Hicks and Del Costa. I was sure Benny was in another room in the building, probably with Hicks.

"Once I blabbed I was gonna take Benny with me, so I could control him. But he jumped the gun. Got there ahead of me."

"And executed two men he thought shot the Don."

"He didn't execute them," I said. "When he went in they went for their Uzis."

"You say."

"What's the bartender say?"

"He ducked behind the bar when Benny came in with a gun."

"Benny says he pulled his gun when the two Jamaicans went for theirs."

"Of course that's what he'd say."

"Look," I said, "they had Uzis, and they'd been braggin' about takin' out a Mafia Don."

"We're checking on that," she said. "Talking to the bartender, other customers. Meanwhile . . ."

"You've got to let us go."

"I can let you go," she said. "I don't know about Benny."

"While you investigate," I said. "He's not goin' anywhere. Not with the Don in the hospital."

She stood up.

"Take his gun, sure," I said. "But he's got a permit for it."

"It's up to Hicks," she said. "I'll talk to him about it."

As she left I wondered where the girl I had met with at Last Exit had gone—or if she had ever really existed?

About a half hour later Hicks came in. He had two containers of coffee. He set one in front of me, then sat across from me with the other one. I removed the plastic lid, found it black. The way I liked it.

"Thanks."

"Sure."

I sipped.

"You're not gettin' the treatment you expected from Del Costa, are you?"

"I'm getting what I'd expect from a cop."

He leaned forward.

"But not from a cop you slept with, huh?"

I didn't say anything. He sat back.

"You're surprised I know about it? I know about all her fuck buddies. Did you think you were special?"

"No," I said. "Not special."

"The bartender says you came after the shootin'," Hicks said. "That means I'm gonna let you go."

"And Benny?"

"I can hold him a while longer," Hicks said. "I'm gonna do that, just to be a nutbuster." He laughed.

"When do I get out?" I asked.

"As soon as you finish your coffee," Hicks said. "And sign your statement."

"What statement?"

"It's bein' typed up."

"I didn't write a statement."

"Del Costa's writin' it up from what you said," Hicks said. "If you don't like it, you don't have to sign it."

I nodded, drank some more coffee.

"I thought we were gonna work together on this, Delvecchio."

"I thought I was gonna stay out of it."

He laughed again.

"I never expected that," he said. "Not from you, Nick. Del Costa thinks you knew where those Jamaicans were and didn't tell us."

"I told her—"

"I know what you told her," Hicks said. "If you hear any other news, you'll let us know first, right?"

"Yes."

"Yeah, you will."

We drank our coffee.

"I'll let your friend Benny out tomorrow," Hicks said, "unless I hear somethin' in the meantime from witnesses."

"The bartender was the only witness," I reminded him, "and he ducked down behind the bar."

"Well, we're still canvassing the area," Hicks said. "We might find somebody else who saw somethin'. If not, I'll let him out."

I finished my coffee, put the empty container on the table. At that moment Del Costa walked in and put my statement down in front of me. Amazingly, what she'd written sounded as if I'd written it myself. I signed it.

"Okay, Nick," Hicks said, "you can go."

Del Costa had nothing to say.

"You goin' to the hospital?" Hicks asked.

"That's right."

"In case you're interested," he said, "the Don is still hangin' on."

"Thanks."

"Of course," Hicks said, "he could move on to his eternal reward before Benny gets out."

At the door I said, "For your sake, I hope not."

Sixty-Seven

WHEN I GOT BACK TO THE HOSPITAL BOTH JACOBY AND PO WERE THERE.

"What happened to working in shifts?" I asked.

Jacoby shrugged. "We figured with you and Benny gone we might as well both stay."

"What happened?" Po asked.

I told them.

"What the fuck," Po said. "The big guy blew it."

"You think he went there planning to kill them?" Jacoby asked.

"I hope not," I said. "I hope it went the way he said it did."

"What did the Don have to say to you this morning?" Jacoby asked.

"Nothin'," I said. "He called my name, and then said that word again."

"Vendetta?" Po asked.

I nodded.

"It's like that's all he can think of."

"Maybe it is," Po said.

"I'm gonna go in for a minute," I said. "In case he can understand, I want to tell him that Benny'll be back."

They nodded.

Inside was quiet, except for the beep of the machines. I walked to his bed and looked down at him. My feelings were mixed. I didn't want him to die, but I wanted to yell at him, "Why didn't you ever tell me!"

I've never been one of those sons who doesn't look at his parents as people. And especially given the business I'm in, I could understand if my parents had marital problems at one time and my mother went looking for solace in the Don's arms. After all, he was always around. Maybe they felt they were protecting me as a child, but once I reached my adulthood, I would like to have known who my real father was.

"Benny should be back tomorrow," I told the unconscious man. "He's out . . . checkin' on somethin' for me. We're workin' together to find out who shot you. You're probably happy to hear me and the big guy are working' together. Funny, I always thought you probably looked at Benny like a son. And maybe you did. Maybe you saw us both as your sons. I don't know. I'm still kinda confused by the whole thing. Maybe you could do me a favor and pull out of this so you can tell me the real story? Is that too much to ask? Just don't die, because I don't know how I'd be able to handle losing two fathers at the same time."

Okay, so much for talking to an unconscious man. They say people can still hear you when they're like that, or in a coma. I didn't know if that was true, but maybe something of what I'd said had gotten through.

I left the room, was saying goodbye to Po and Jacoby when I saw Sam running down the hall towards me. She had obviously dressed in a hurry. Her hair was in tangle and tears were streaming down her face.

"Nick, Nick" she said, breathlessly. She reached and gripped my upper arms with surprising strength. "I didn't know where else to look for you."

"What's wrong?" I asked.

"It's . . . it's . . . something's happened at your father's house. Vinnie called. He said . . . he said . . . Nick, it's Maria."

"What?"

"Something happened to your sister."

"Watch him," I said to my two friends. "Watch him like a hawk!"

I grabbed Sam's arm and we ran.

We couldn't get near the house. The street was blocked off not only by police vehicles, but by fire trucks and cars.

The sky was filled with black smoke.

"Jesus," I said, as we got out of the car.

I started running, avoiding cops, firemen, vehicles, barricades, until two uniformed cops grabbed me and stopped me before I could get to the house, which was ablaze.

"Hold on, fella," one of them said.

"That's my house," I said. "My father's house."

"It's okay," somebody said. "Let him go."

I turned my head, saw Vinnie coming toward me. He was covered with soot, which made his white collar stand out.

"He's my brother," he said to the two cops.

They let go, but one of them—the older one—said, "Take it easy, pal. You can't go runnin' in there."

Vinnie grabbed my arm.

"He's right, Nick," Vinnie said. "I tried . . . I tried to get inside."

"Vinnie," I said, "Maria, where's Maria?"

He looked at me, eyes streaming with tears and said, "Inside, Nick. Maria was inside."

Sixty-Eight

FATHER VINNIE WANTED ME TO PRAY, BUT I REFUSED. AFTER ALL, WHAT kind of God takes my father, and then my sister?

We stayed as long as we could. They managed to extinguish the fire, but it was going to take some time for things to cool down enough for them to go in and look for bodies. Until then, I could hold out hope that maybe Maria wasn't inside the house.

According to the cops and the witnesses, they heard an explosion, and then the house just went up.

"Could be a lot of things," the Fire Chief said. "Could've been the hot water heater, or a gas explosion . . ."

Yeah, I thought, or a Molotov cocktail tossed in a window.

I had just one word running through my mind at that moment.

Vendetta!

I told Vinnie what had happened that morning with Benny and the Jamaicans.

"That sounds crazy," he said. "Why would Benny go there to kill them? You needed at least one of them alive to find out who put them up to it."

"He says he had no choice."

"Do you believe him?"

I shrugged.

"When I pulled up in front I heard the Uzi fire, and then single shots, probably from Benny's forty-five. So yeah, I think they fired first."

"But?"

"But . . . I don't know. He says he didn't pull his gun until they fired, but if he rushed in with his gun in his hand . . ."

" . . . then he instigated the exchange."

"Yeah."

"Well, Nick, going all the way back to high school Benny was never the sharpest knife in the drawer."

"I know that, Vin."

It was a surreal scene. My father's house reduced to rubble, the two of us standing there, discussing the case while waiting for our sister's body to be carried out.

Sam was standing off to the side, arms folded, probably unsure what to do. Should she stay, should she go? Should she try to talk to us? Vinnie had called her when he couldn't get me, and she'd promised she'd find me.

I walked over to her, took her by the upper arms.

"You should go home."

"No," she said. "I'll stay."

"Vinnie and I are gonna stay until . . . until they bring her out."

"Maybe," she said, "maybe she's not in there."

I took her hand.

"That's what we're hoping."

She squeezed my hand and said, "I'll stay."

It was hours later, dark out, the street lit by portable lights, when two firemen wheeled her body out on a stretcher. She was zipped into a body bag.

"Stay here," I said to Vinnie.

"I have to give her last rites," he said. He took his stole from his pocket.

"Okay." I turned to Sam. "Wait here."

She hugged herself and nodded.

We walked over.

"Are you sure you want to do this?" the Fire Chief asked.

"I'm sure we have to," I said.

He nodded to his men and they unzipped the body bag.

She was too burned for us to tell it was her, but there was a ring on her finger that we both knew.

"Is it her?" the Chief asked.

"Looks like it," I said. "That's her ring. But the M.E. will have to tell us."

Vinnie put the stole around his neck and gave her the last rites, then nodded for them to take her away.

"Come on, Vin," I said. "Let's go."

We turned, and I saw Sergeant Hicks and Detective Del Costa standing by Sam. Vinnie and I walked over.

"We heard about it over the air," Hicks said. "We're sorry for your loss."

"Thanks."

"Do you think this has any connection to your father's death?"

I shrugged. I was shaking inside, and trying to hold it together.

"No way to tell now," I said. "We'll have to let everybody do their jobs, tell us how the fire started, tell us if it's really her."

"Then maybe you should all go home," Hicks said, "and let us do our jobs."

"Yeah," I said, "maybe we should."

I looked at Del Costa, whose face was expressionless.

"Come on, Sam," I said. "Let's take Vinnie back with us."

"I'll talk to the local detectives," Hicks said.

I looked at him, wondering why he was being so helpful.

"Okay," I said. "If they want to talk to me later just let me know."

"Go on," he said, "take your brother home."

The three of us walked back to my car. I didn't know if Vinnie had driven himself or not, but he wasn't talking. Ever since he completed the last rites he hadn't said a word. In fact, his stole was still around his neck.

Sam got in the back seat with him and I drove away from the site.

"Nick," he said, finally.

"Yeah?"

"Take me to the Rectory."

"Are you sure, Vin? Maybe you should come home with me—"

"No," he said, "you have work to do. You have to find out who did this. And I have arrangements to make. And my own job to do."

"Vinnie—"

"The Rectory," he said.

"Okay, Vinnie," I said, "Okay."

Sixty-Nine

WE DROPPED VINNIE AT THE RECTORY. BEFORE HE WENT INSIDE HE TURNED and gripped my hand.

"Do what you have to do, Nick," he said. "And be who you have to be."

Then he ran down the steps to the front door.

"What did he mean by that?" Sam asked.

"I'm not sure," I said.

I drove us home.

We walked down the hall to our apartment doors. At least, I thought we were, but Sam didn't stop at hers. She walked with me to mine.

"I'm coming in with you," she said. "You shouldn't be alone tonight."

I didn't argue with her. I was too damned drained. I unlocked the door and we went inside. I walked to the sofa and sat down. Sam went to the kitchen and came back with two beers.

"Unless you want whiskey?" she asked.

"No," I said, taking the green bottle from her, "this is fine."

She sat down next to me.

"Maybe it's not her, Nick," she said.

"We'll find out tomorrow," I said, "but who else could it be?"

"A neighbor, maybe?" she asked. "Somebody who came over to talk to Maria. Maybe your sister went out to the grocery store?"

"There was still plenty of food in the frig," I said. "besides, if she went shopping where is she now?"

Sam shrugged helplessly.

"Look, Sam, I appreciate the company," I said, "but I really do need to be alone, to think."

"You're going to work tonight?"

"I need to find out if this has anything to do with my dad bein' shot, and the Don."

"Are you going out?"

"I don't know," I said. "I just need some time."

She put her hand on my back.

"You'll call me if you need me?"

"You can count on it."

"Nick—" she said, putting her arms around me. I buried my face in her hair and breathed her in. It would have been very easy for me to just stay like that, but I reluctantly pulled away.

"Thanks for goin' with me, Sam."

She nodded, put down her beer, and stood up. Maybe I was a fool to let her walk out, but I did, and then I was alone. I finished my beer, and hers, while I sat there and tried to figure out my next move.

Vendetta.

That was all I could think about. It was pretty much all the Don was able to say from his hospital bed. If there was someone out there who knew I was the Don's blood, then I was included in the Vendetta. And if I was included, then anyone related to me by blood was, too.

They had killed my father, and Maria.

And that left Vinnie.

And I had dropped him at the Rectory, alone.

I couldn't afford to wait for an autopsy to tell me if the dead girl in the fire actually was my sister. I had to save my brother.

Seventy

I DROVE THROUGH THE STREETS OF BROOKLYN LIKE A MADMAN, TAKING the shortest route I knew, ignoring traffic lights and stop signs. Rehearsing my story for when I got stopped by cops.

But I never did.

At that moment, if Vinnie was right and there was a God, he was looking over me, helping me to get to Father Vinnie in time.

I had tried calling the Rectory, but at that time of night no one answered.

I stopped my car in front of the Rectory and rushed to the door. It was locked, so I pounded on it, and rang the bell. Eventually, a sleepy Priest answered the door with a less than priestly look on his face.

"What in God's name—" he said.

"Father Vincent, where is he?"

"Now look here—"

"I'm his brother," I said. "I need to see him . . . now!"

I pushed past him to the stairway, up to Vinnie's room. The door was locked.

The Priest came in behind me.

"It's locked," I said. "Do you have a key?"

"What are you doing?" he demanded.

"What's going on?" another man asked, coming down the hall.

"Monsignor, this man burst through the door—"

The priest was white-haired, in his sixties. The Monsignor was a younger man by at least ten years, his head bald with a fringe of gray around. They were both wearing robes—expensive robes. That fact was one of the reasons I didn't like the Church.

"I need to get into Father Vinnie's room," I said. "I'm his brother, Nick."

"Yes, I recognize you," the Monsignor said, "but why are you here this late—"

"Monsignor," I said. "My brother is in danger. I need to get inside." I threw my shoulder into the door, but it was solid and hardly budged.

"I need a key!" I shouted at them.

"Yes, yes, all right," the Monsignor said. "Just a minute."

He went to his room, I assumed to get his keys. I tried the door again with my shoulder, but it was thick and well built. Expensive, damn it. Carvings on the outside.

"How do these doors lock?" I asked the old priest. "From the inside."

"Or the outside," he said. "You just have to pull it closed behind you when you leave."

The Monsignor reappeared.

"Hurry!"

He turned on the light in the hall, started going through the keys on his ring.

"Hurry up!"

"I've got it," he said. "I've got it."

He leaned over the door and slid the key into the lock. When he turned it he stepped back and I pushed through, into the room.

Vinnie was on the floor.

Bleeding.

Dying.

He had his hands over his belly, ribbons of blood flowing from between them. He looked up at me.

"Nick," he said, "oh Nick."

"Vinnie!"

I ran to him, got on the floor, took him into my arms, trying not to jar him.

"Call nine-one-one!" I shouted at the two stunned priests. "Call an ambulance!"

The old priest withdrew from the room. The Monsignor continued to stare for a few second, then also backed out. He returned with his stole around his neck, and knelt by us.

"No!" I said.

"I must give him last rites."

"No! You can't!" I looked down at Vinnie's face. He was pale, so pale. "Vinnie, who did it? Who did this to you?"

The Monsignor started to drone on, praying, gesturing.

"Come on, Vinnie," I said, clutching him to me. "Hang on."

He moved one of his hands and I took it, sticky with his blood. He squeezed my hand tightly.

"That's it," I said, "that's it. Squeeze, and keep squeezing." I looked up. "Damn it, where's that ambulance."

I reached up to the bed, pulled a pillow from it and tried to press it over his belly, tried to staunch the flow of blood. I didn't know how bad the wound was, but if I could just stop the bleeding.

"Vinnie," I said, "Vin, who did it?"

"Nick," he whispered.

"What? What is it?"

I lowered my head so that my ear was almost to his mouth.

"Nick," he whispered, "Nicky."

And he stopped squeezing my hand.

Seventy-One

I WATCHED AS THEY CARRIED MY BROTHER'S BODY OUT OF THE RECTORY ON a stretcher. The ambulance had arrived, too late, and then the police.

And then Hicks and Del Costa.

I was sitting in a small room of the Rectory, where couples waited for their counseling appointments, or to arrange a wedding, a baptism—or a funeral mass. Where they waited to hear words of comfort from the men who served God—or claimed to.

God!

I had thought God was protecting me as I drove through those red lights and stop signs. Protecting me so I could get to my brother and save him. But no. He was protecting me so I could get there in time for my brother to die in my arms.

God damn you, I thought, and then started to laugh because I realized how silly that was. God wasn't about to damn himself. Not when he could have his fun damning all of us.

I looked up, saw Hicks and Del Costa staring at me, probably wondering if I had lost my mind. At least this time the lady detective who had shared my bed one night had the good grace to look sad.

"You're the last one in your family left, Delvecchio," Hicks said. "Maybe you should tell us what the hell is goin' on?"

"I thought he was out of his head," I said. "It seemed like the only word he could remember."

"What are you talkin' about?" Hicks demanded.

"The Don," I said. "Every time he wakes up he says the same word—'Vendetta.'"

"You're tellin' me all these killings are the result of some wacky Italian Vendetta?"

"I'm not tellin' you that," I said. "The Don told me, and now . . ." I stopped, shook my head, too choked up to finish.

"And now what?" Hicks said. "Come on, Delvecchio. Spit it out! Mourn on your own time."

I glared at him through tears and said, "Just before my brother died in my arms he looked at me and said 'Vendetta.'"

"Goddamit!" Hicks said. "This ain't a damned Godfather movie!"

"Look, what can I tell you?" I asked. "My father, sister and brother are dead. If you think there's another connection, find it. Do your job!"

Hicks pointed his index finger at me.

"I been coddlin' you because you been losin' family," he said, "and my partner's been pushin' me, but no more."

"Well, I've got no more family to give, Sergeant Hicks," I said. "All I've got left are the Don, and probably Benny."

And maybe Sam, but I didn't even want to say that out loud.

"You tellin' me you're related to Benny Carbone?" he asked.

"No, I'm not related to him. Just do him a favor and keep him in your jail."

"Too late for that," Hicks said. "I cut him loose hours ago."

Was Benny in danger? I wondered. He was close to the Don, but he wasn't blood.

"Why would a Vendetta against the Barracuda include you and your family?" he demanded. "What the hell are you hidin'?"

I bit my tongue.

"Is he more than your godfather?" Hicks demanded. "Your uncle, maybe?"

I still wasn't ready to admit that the Don was my father. Not to Hicks, anyway.

"I should take you in," Hicks said.

I looked down at my hands.

"For what?" I asked. "For being covered in my brother's blood?"

He didn't take me in, not that I cared much, at that moment. He and Del Costa left and I sat there a few more minutes, trying to process everything that had happened that night, until the Monsignor and the old priest came up to me.

"Is there something we can do for you, my son?" the Monsignor asked, solicitously.

"Yeah," I said, standing up, "get the fuck away from me."

He flinched like I'd slapped him.

"You and your God," I added. "Just stay the hell away from me!"

Seventy-Two

THEY WERE ALL GONE.

My whole family.

If the Don was my father, then he was the last one left—but he was also the reason they were all dead.

I headed for the hospital.

Visiting hours were long over, but I didn't let that stop me. I walked into the place like I belonged there and took the elevator to the Don's floor. When I saw the crowd, I knew I was too late. It had all gone down in one night.

I hurried down the hall, was met by both Po and Jacoby.

"We're sorry, Nick," Jacoby said.

"What happened?"

"He just . . . died," Po said.

"What?"

"They're saying it happens," Jacoby said. "A patient seems to be doing okay, and then . . ."

"He wasn't killed?"

"No, Nick," Po said. "He just died. Why? What's going on?"

I told them.

"Jesus," Jacoby said, "my God, I'm so sorry."

"Yeah," Po said. "What the hell is going on, Nick?"

"Vendetta," I said.

"That again?" Jacoby asked.

"It's the only explanation," I said. "It's what my brother said before he died. Whether I really am the Don's son or not, somebody obviously thinks so. And my blood is his blood."

"And you're the last one left," Jacoby said.

"Nick," Po said, "you've got to get out of town."

"I can't—"

"You have to," Jacoby said. "Whoever's doing this is determined. Hell, they got your brother *in* the Rectory!"

I couldn't think about leaving town and running. I had to find out for sure what happened to the Don.

I moved past Po and Jacoby and headed for the room. As I reached the door it opened and Benny came out.

"Benny, what the hell—" I said.

"He's gone, Nick," he said. "The Don's gone."

I talked with the doctor. He repeated what Jacoby had told me. "Sometimes it happens."

"Doctor, he couldn't have been killed?"

The Doctor frowned.

"He was a very sick man, Mr. Delvecchio," he said. "This is not an unusual situation. I feel no compulsion to notify the police that his death may be suspicious."

"That's okay, Doc," I said. "There'll be an autopsy, anyway, just because of who he was, and why he was in here."

"That may be," the doctor said, "but my job is done."

He walked away. I thought about going into the Don's room to look at him, then thought, why bother? Dead is dead. He may have been my real father, but my whole family was dead because of something he had done in his past.

And I might still die as a result of it.

I walked down the hall to where Benny was seated, and Po and Jacoby were standing. I told them to go home.

"You need us to watch your back, Nick," Jacoby said.

"Go home," I said. "You're done. I appreciate your help, but I can't have you around me. I don't want to be responsible for any more deaths."

"Nick," Po said, "you're not responsible for any of this."

"I appreciate that, Hank," I said. "Go home, both of you . . . please."

Po turned and headed for the elevator. Jacoby put his hand on my arm and said. "Get out of town, Nick. Run. At least until this all blows over."

As he joined Po in the elevator I wondered if Vendettas ever really blew over? Didn't they just go on until everybody was dead?

I walked over to Benny, who looked up at me through bloodshot eyes.

"There was nothin' I could do, Nick," he said. "I mean, I'm a strong guy, and I can shoot, but . . . there was nothin' . . ."

"I know, Benny," I said, patting him on the shoulder. "I know."

"The dicks told me about your family," he said. "I'm so sorry."

"Yeah, thanks."

"I don't know what to do now," Nick," he said. "What're you gonna do?"

"I don't know, Benny."

"Maybe," Benny said, "we should work together, find the people who killed your family."

I thought about what he'd done to the two Jamaicans. And who would we look for? Italians, or a Russian killer working for Italians?

"I don't think you should be near me, Benny," I said. "I don't think anybody should be near me."

"Nick—"

"You've got the Don's business to take care of, Benny," I said.

"But you," he said, "you're his—"

"Nobody was more his son than you, Benny," I said. "You take care of it. And take care of yourself."

"Nicky—" he said, but I walked to the elevator which—thankfully—opened at that moment. I stepped in and rode down.

Epilogue

Somewhere in the Midwest, 2010

1

"I RAN, AND ENDED UP HERE," I FINISHED.

The three men had listened to my story, two of them with bored looks on their faces, but the spokesman, he looked very interested the whole time.

"That's some story," the spokesman said.

"Answer your questions?" I asked.

"Most of 'em."

"Why so interested?"

Before he could answer he cocked his head, put the fingers of his left hand to his ear. Obviously he had an earpiece there.

"Yep, we're in. Yes, you can come up."

"Somebody else arrived?" I asked.

"My boss."

"You guys aren't cops," I said. "Not Feds. Mafia?"

They all snorted.

"There's no more Mafia, Mr. Delvecchio," the spokesman said.

We all waited and I heard the gravel crunch again beneath the tires of a vehicle. I could see enough of it to tell it was a stretch Hummer. But I couldn't see who was getting out, so I leaned forward, careful not to let the gun I was sitting on slip to the floor.

I caught my breath.

Benny.

And it all clicked into place, fifteen years later.

Benny, in the restaurant when the Uzi strafed the Don and Vito Delvecchio;

Benny, rushing ahead of me to gun down the two Jamaicans;

Benny, not in custody when Maria and Vinnie were killed;

Benny, alone with the Don when he died.

Benny . . . not as dumb as he made out to be.

The driver stayed by the car while Benny walked up onto the deck. I sat back in my chair, comforted by the gun under my left buttocks.

"Hey, Nicky."

"Benny."

There was a look in his eyes I had never seen. Benny had always had street smarts, but now he looked . . . almost intelligent. Also, he'd gone to fat over the years, was a lot wider than he used to be. His hair was gray and thinning.

"You look good, Nick," he said. "Ain't aged much. Still got your hair."

"Can't say the same for you," I said. "You're fat and bald."

He didn't like that, but he shook it off.

"You don't look surprised to see me."

"I was surprised when the door opened and you stepped out," I said, "but then it all made sense."

"It did, huh?"

"You were alone with the Don," I said. "What'd you do, pinch off his oxygen?"

"Actually, that made it easy. They had just put him on oxygen that morning, because his breathing started to labor."

"So let me guess," I said. "There was no Vendetta."

Benny made a rude sound with his mouth.

"That's goombah stuff, Nicky. But all I had to do was keep whisperin' that word in the Don's ear while he was unconscious. Every time he woke up, he said it."

"And killin' Maria and Father Vinnie?"

"Supported the idea of a Vendetta," Benny said. "Kept the cops—and you—off balance. Nobody ever looked at me."

"And why kill the Don in the first place?" I asked.

"He let it slip a couple of years before that you were his son," Benny said. "Right then I knew I wasn't gettin' nothin'. You would get it all. So I started to plan."

"The Jamaicans?"

"A couple of idiots I had use for. The one thing I'm sorry about was your dad. I mean Vito. I never wanted him to get killed."

"But you did," I said. "Your sniper hit him right in the heart."

He chuckled, which made me want to choke him with my bare hands.

"Yeah well, in the end I figured that'd confuse the cops, too. Who was the target? The Don? Vito?"

"It was a good plan, Benny," I said. "Confused everybody. Frustrated the hell out of me. Tell me something."

"What?"

"You didn't somehow mess with the blood test results, did you?"

"Nope," he said. "I had nothin' to do with that. You really were the Don's son."

"And that's really why you're here, fifteen years later?" I asked.

"I never thought you'd run, Nicky," he said. "I thought we had time to kill you. But you disappeared."

"And you've been lookin' for me all these years?"

"On and off. When I'd hear somethin' about a job bein' done that sounded like you, I'd send somebody to have a look."

"This guy?" I asked, indicating the spokesman.

"Usually. He's my number one."

"He's not Italian."

"There's no more family, Nick," Benny said. "I run my own shop."

"But you started with everything the Don had, right?"

"True. His cash, he had some investments, I sold the Barge . . . he left me everything, but only in the event you weren't around."

"So now what?"

"Well," Benny said, "I can't have you ever comin' back and claimin' your birthright."

"I don't want it, Benny."

"So you say," Benny said. "But I'm makin' sure. That's how I got where I am—makin' sure."

"So where's your shooter?" I asked. "He out in the trees with a Russian sniper rifle?"

"I don't need shooter for this, Nick," he said. "I never liked you. Did you know that?"

"You know, Benny," I said. "I always thought you were even dumber than you seemed."

Benny chuckled, shook his head, and reached leisurely into his jacket for his gun. Still a .45. I saw that just before I raised my left hand and shot him in the chest.

Talk about surprised.

2

Following my shot the sound of the hammer being cocked above their head attracted the other three men. As Benny slumped to the deck they looked up at Sam, pointing a 9-mm Glock at them. She was holding it with both hands, the way I taught her. The three men paused with their hands chest high, ready to reach into their jackets.

The spokesman looked at me.

"What's it gonna be?" I asked. "Your boss is dead. The empire is up for grabs."

"He really wasn't very smart."

I shrugged.

"You really aren't going to come back?" he asked.

"No."

"Is she any good with that Glock?"

"Very good."

He waved at the other two men to put their hands down.

"Take him with you," I said. "There's an ordinance around here about burying dead animals on your own property."

"Pick him up," he said to the others.

"He's heavy, Alexei."

Alexei made an annoyed face as the man spoke his name.

"Get Harry to help you."

They waved to the driver, who came warily up the steps, took stock of the situation, and then helped the two men carry Benny off the deck.

"Good luck to you," Alexei said, and started to turn.

"Alexei."

He stopped.

I stood up.

"That's Russian, right?"

"I was hoping you wouldn't catch that."

"The sniper," I said. "You killed my father. And Carlo."

"It was my job."

"And my sister and brother?"

"Still my job. Benny paid me."

"And that made you his number one."

He was half turned. I couldn't see his hand, but Sam could.

"Tell me something, Mr. Delvecchio," Alexei said.

"What?"

"That horse you gave Winky money to bet for you?" he asked. "What did it do?"

"It won," I said. "Paid Fifty-five dollars. I picked up the money from him before we left town. I needed every cent I had."

"Guess you're pretty good with longshots."

"Not typically."

"I don't suppose you'll let me walk off this deck."

"Not likely."

"I didn't think so. You know, it was nothing personal."

"Sorry I can't say the same."

He nodded and went into his jacket for his gun. Sam and I fired at the same time. Alexei went down, his gun flying out of his hand and off the deck.

The three men carrying Benny dropped him and ran up the stairs. Sam and I had them covered.

"Put Benny in the car, come back for Alexei," I said. "Then leave."

They looked at me, then Sam, then at each other. In the end they put Benny in the back seat, and Alexei in the trunk. Then they sent one last look our way before getting into the car and leaving.

Sam came down from the upper deck, the gun hanging limply from her shaking hands. I took it from her, and gave her a hug.

"Did I hit him?" she asked.

"I killed him," I said. "But you probably saved us."

"Should I pack?" she asked. "Again?"

"Afraid so."

"Shit," she said. "I liked it here."

"Me, too."

"Another new address for my agent."

After leaving Brooklyn with me Sam had been writing her books under all different names, depending on her agent to sell them on their merit. We couldn't afford for her to keep using the same name.

She probably shouldn't have been writing at all, but once she agreed to leave Brooklyn with me I couldn't ask her to give up what she loved.

"Someday," I said, "you'll be able to come out from behind all the pen names."

She squeezed me around the waist and said, "Oh, I complain, but I don't care. As long as we're together."

"Better get packed," I said, kissing her.

She went to the door, then stopped.

"Nick?"

"Yeah?"

"With Benny dead, and the Russian who killed your family, what about . . ."

"We can't go back to Brooklyn, Sam," I said. "It was the end of Brooklyn for us a long time ago. We can't change now."

"I know," she said. "I know."

I didn't really care about Brooklyn, anymore. There was nothing there for me. All the family I had left was Sam, and as long as she was with me, I was home.

About the Author

Robert J. Randisi, founder of the Private Eye Writers of America, is a publishing phenomenon. With more than five hundred novels under his belt, he shows no sign of slowing down. His latest work includes several books for Perfect Crime: a short-story collection, *The Guilt Edge*; two novels, *The End of Brooklyn* and *The Bottom of Every Bottle*; and *The Shamus Winners*, a two-volume compilation of more than twenty-five years' worth of prize-winning private-eye stories.

Described by *Booklist* as "the last of the pulp writers," Randisi has published in the western, mystery, horror, science fiction and men's adventure genres. In 2009, he received the PWA's Lifetime Achievement Award.

Randisi was born and raised in Brooklyn, N.Y., and from 1973 through 1981 he was a civilian employee of the New York City Police Department, working out of the Sixty-Seventh Precinct in Brooklyn. After forty-one years in New York, he now resides in Clarksville, Missouri, an artisan community of five hundred people. He lives and works with writer Marthayn Pelegrimas in a small house on three acres, with a deck that overlooks the Mississippi.

If you enjoyed this book, look for these other titles by Robert J. Randisi published by PERFECT CRIME BOOKS.

THE GUILT EDGE
232 pages. $12.95. ISBN: 978-0-9825157-3-0

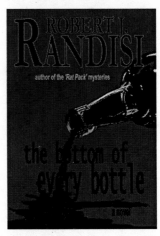

THE BOTTOM OF EVERY BOTTLE
186 pages. $12.95. ISBN: 978-09825157-1-6

THE SHAMUS WINNERS VOLUME I (1982-1995)
336 PAGES. $14.95. ISBN: 978-0-9825157-4-7

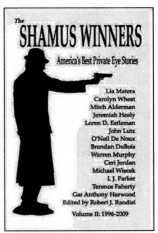

THE SHAMUS WINNERS VOLUME II (1996-2009)
282 pages. $14.95. ISBN: 978-0-9825157-6-1

Available at bookstores, Amazon, and at ww.PerfectCrimeBooks.com

CPSIA information can be obtained at www.ICGtesting.com
Printed in the USA
LVOW091913061011

249428LV00001B/94/P